A VIKING NOVEL
OF
MYSTERY
AND
SUSPENSE

BY JOHN WILLIAM CORRINGTON AND JOYCE H. CORRINGTON

So Small a Carnival

A Project Named Desire

A Civil Death

ALSO BY JOHN WILLIAM CORRINGTON

POETRY

Where We Are

Mr. Clean and Other Poems

The Anatomy of Love

Lines to the South

FICTION

And Wait for the Night

The Upper Hand

The Lonesome Traveler and Other Stories

The Bombardier

The Actes and Monuments

The Southern Reporter

Shad Sentell

All My Trials

The Collected Stories of John William Corrington

EDITED WITH MILLER WILLIAMS

Southern Writing in the Sixties: Fiction

Southern Writing in the Sixties: Poetry

THE WHITE ZONE

by JOHN WILLIAM CORRINGTON
and JOYCE H. CORRINGTON

VIKING

VIKING
Published by the Penguin Group
Viking Penguin, a division of Penguin Books USA Inc.,
375 Hudson Street, New York, New York 10014, U.S.A.
Penguin Books Ltd, 27 Wrights Lane,
London W8 5TZ, England
Penguin Books Australia Ltd, Ringwood,
Victoria, Australia
Penguin Books Canada Ltd, 2801 John Street,
Markham, Ontario, Canada L3R 1B4
Penguin Books (N.Z.) Ltd, 182–190 Wairau Road,
Auckland 10, New Zealand

Penguin Books Ltd, Registered Offices:
Harmondsworth, Middlesex, England

First published in 1990 by Viking Penguin,
a division of Penguin Books USA Inc.

1 3 5 7 9 10 8 6 4 2

LIBRARY OF CONGRESS CATALOGING IN PUBLICATION DATA
Corrington, John William.
The white zone / by John William Corrington and Joyce H. Corrington.
p. cm.
ISBN 0-670-82229-9
I. Corrington, Joyce H. II. Title.
PS3553.07W4 1990
813'.54—dc20 89-40807

Printed in the United States of America
Set in Times Roman
Designed by Wilma Jane Weichselbaum

A. M. D. G.

and

in memory of
John William Corrington
(1932–1988)

We held one another for ten thousand millennia,
cycle after cycle passing around us,
the flux finding new variations on its
single game, play, show, each time a thread
wound down to what seemed, had to be,
its mortal end. Then she said:
—I love you. I always have. I always will.

—John William Corrington
"The Risi's Wife"

THE WHITE ZONE

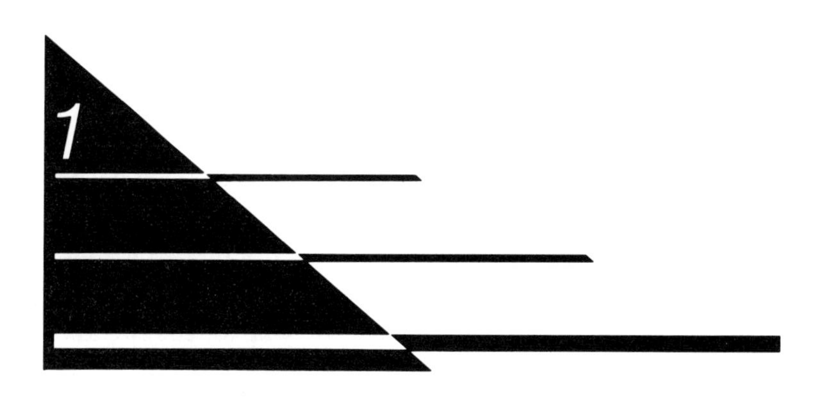

My plane was late. I was already overdue down on Hollywood Boulevard when it landed. A nice freckle-faced redhead with splendid legs and a cute ass, dressed in a miniskirted chauffeur's outfit, met me at the gate holding up a hand-lettered sign that said TRAPP.

—I'm Leslie, my luscious driver told me even before I could ask. —Welcome to Los Angeles. Have you been here before, Mr. Trapp?

—Once or twice. Toting.

—Uh . . . toting?

—Toting a prisoner out here, or toting one back to New Orleans.

—Oh, you're a police officer?

—A captain of Homicide. New Orleans Police Department.

She gave me a wide-eyed look, then left to go fetch the car while I collected my luggage.

—The White Zone is for loading and unloading only. No stopping, a male voice said as I stood at curbside.

—The White Zone is for loading and unloading only. No stopping, a female voice whispered in reply.

Then the recorded voices said the same thing again, and they repeated it once more, and they kept warning each other over and over till I got the notion that there was something deeper in those words than keeping traffic moving at LAX—maybe a message to a black Homicide cop visiting from New Orleans.

You get to thinking crazy and paranoid in my business. See, I'd been wading in blood all summer, praying for cool weather or common sense, whichever come first. From May till September, it had been what we call 90/90 in New Orleans. That's temperature and humidity, and when it hits in that region and stays there a week or so, the murder rate goes through the ceiling. Husbands knifing wives, wives setting husbands on fire. Poker buddies using the kids' Boy Scout hatchets on one another.

I'd put in five months of almost steady overtime before the first cool front come through in October. Then, like another breath of fresh air, Camille Bynum had phoned.

—Ralph . . .

Without another word, I knew it was her. Nobody but my dead momma and Camille ever called me by my given name. Besides, I knew her warm, rich voice. The sound of it whispering my name had haunted my dreams for twenty years.

Camille and me went back as far as you can go. The two of us grew up living and loving together in New Orleans' Desire project. That's the biggest public housing project in the world. Twenty thousand black people jammed into a few square blocks. In the sixties it wasn't the hellhole of dope and hopelessness it's gotten to be. But even then it was a dead-end kind of life, and both of us wanted out. We wanted that bright future the Movement was promising us was gonna be ours with the next demonstration, the next court victory.

I always figured we'd find it together. Only Camille took a shortcut. She left me and Desire riding in a big white Cadillac, sitting next to a rich white bastard.

That sonofabitch was dead and buried now. But I guess Camille had gotten most of what she went looking for. She was living in a big mansion in West L.A. and no doubt driving her own white Cadillac or Mercedes or Rolls or whatever it took to make a beautiful black girl feel at home in the White Zone.

Camille and me had talked on that phone for maybe an hour or more. And the next day I told Major Mauvais I needed me some rest time. He agreed and offered me the use of his fishing camp down on Lake Borgne. But I'd made other plans.

Camille wanted me to join her in L.A. She sent me a first-class airline ticket and a car to pick me up at LAX.

That cute red-headed driver finally pulled up to the curb at the wheel of a silver gray Rolls-Royce. I tossed my bag in the back seat, got in beside it. Leslie watched me curiously in the rearview mirror as I unpacked my Colt Cobra and slipped it into my shoulder holster.

—It'll be a half-hour drive into Hollywood, Captain Trapp. Just make yourself comfortable.

That'd be easy to do. Priciest car I'd ever owned was a real clean Olds demo that went for twelve thousand. Now here I was in the back seat of a little number that pushed 200 thousand even on sale—if they had Rolls-Royce sales. Black leather and oiled, polished mahogany, a little TV and a big bar.

There was an unopened bottle of Black Bush staring back at me. I just had to reach out, break the seal, and pour myself a shot over one ice cube, with a dash of soda. I didn't see where I'd be traveling this way again in the near future. So I sipped away as we headed north toward those towns where all our dreams get assembled: Hollywood, Burbank, Studio City, Universal City.

Camille had asked me to come to L.A. to watch them put one of those stars into the concrete of Hollywood Boulevard for her son, Danny Bynum. Danny had been the lead singer with a rock group called Desire Project. Their last recording went platinum, and it looked for a while like they were gonna give the Beatles and the Stones a run for all-time hits. Till Danny Bynum's death canceled their appearances and sent them all on their separate ways. Normally, I wouldn't have traveled across town to see phony history being slapped into cement, much less to La-La Land. But I hadn't been at Danny's funeral, and I figured I owed his memory some kind of ceremony. See, Camille had taken part of me with her when she left Desire—she'd been pregnant with my son.

I shook off the echo of Danny's last sad song and looked outside the car. Mercedeses and Porsches, Audis, BMWs and more Rollses zipped past us going and coming. The only domestic stuff I saw was Blazers, Jeeps, and a few pickups with sheepskin seatcovers. I could see why the American car industry was doing hard time. Don't nobody drive Olds anymore?

—California has the seventh largest economy in the world, my young lady said, as if I'd asked her. —Our largest export used to be agriculture. Now it's show business.

—Movies?

—And television, music . . .

I guess I nodded and smiled. The seventh biggest economy on the goddamned planet, and what these folks did best with wasn't food or steel or oil. It was entertainment.

My cute girl driver did a left off Sunset this side of a huge supermarket, then a right on Hollywood Boulevard, and we went into a time-warp: Everything in sight was two- or three-story apartments and houses from the late twenties through the thirties—or imitations of them. Somebody in the stucco business must have made a lot of money. The colors were all variations of earth: tans, browns, soft yellows, beiges, off-whites. You could use that piece of the street for a period movie. Hell, they probably had. A dozen times.

Then we come to that part of Hollywood Boulevard where

the action was—or where it used to be back in the thirties. On the right was the Hollywood Roosevelt Hotel, done over and looking all right. On the left, Mann's Chinese Theatre. That's where the stars begin. They got Elvis and Jerry Lee, John Wayne and Glenn Miller, all in the sidewalk, and don't ask me why people by the hundreds come from Decatur and Toledo, Brookline and Laramie, with their little cameras to take pictures of the sidewalks. People do what they do.

On the sidewalk on the far side of the Chinese Theatre, there was a temporary wooden platform with big speakers at the front pointed out toward the crowd that was packed up tight around it. Traffic cops with L.A.P.D. badges on their uniforms were detouring cars down Orange Street because the crowd was already out into Hollywood Boulevard and growing fast.

—I guess I'd better drop you here, Captain Trapp, Leslie said. —I'll park in the Roosevelt lot and pick you up afterward.

—No need. I'm staying at the Roosevelt, I told her.

—Umm, but Mrs. Bynum has reservations at Ma Maison for this evening.

—And you're toting, right?

Leslie turned this movie-premiere-spotlight smile on me. —That's right. I'm . . . toting.

I gave her back the best grin I had, and got out of the car in front of the hotel. The sun was fading in the west, behind saffron-colored clouds, and neon was starting to come on up and down Hollywood Boulevard. Across the street, the platform was brightly lit by floodlights suspended on an overhead metal frame. I could see a camera crew working. Behind them, a row of black stretch limos filled the side street. They'd no doubt brought all the notables who filled the small stage.

Seated on folding chairs up on the platform were a bunch of people dressed every which way: jeans, Hawaiian shirts, sports jackets, business suits. Over the loudspeaker system, a band was playing an instrumental version of "Wise Child," the last song Danny wrote and sang.

It seemed to me I recognized the boys in the band up on the stand. Sure I did. The kids from Desire Project. They had been performing on stage at the Superdome in New Orleans before a crowd of seventy thousand screaming teenagers the night Danny collapsed. Now they were back together for a last gig to honor his memory.

Then the song ended, and some fat man with the style of a game-show host and a voice like my old drill instructor's took over the mike and started going on about Danny Bynum, the new star on the Boulevard. To hear him tell, the eyes of the world were glued to Hollywood. The stars never died, they were just translated—into the sky above L.A., into the pavement of Hollywood Boulevard.

But I wasn't paying much mind to him, because I had spotted Camille. She was sitting in the front row just back of the podium, still looking like she was in her twenties and had never known what trouble meant. She wore a clinging white silk dress that caressed her figure and set off the light chamois color of her skin. Her dark eyes were sweeping the crowd, I guess trying to spot me.

I had hung back at the edge of things till then, but I found myself pushing past people, moving toward her. That old magnetism was still working. Memories of hot nights twenty years ago in her project apartment began stirring. And I thought I'd slammed and locked the door on them the day Camille had left with no word of warning, just a message that we'd meet again somewhere down the road. I'd signed up army the next day, and hadn't come back from Germany for ten years, not till I heard she'd left New Orleans. And all that time, and the ten years since for that matter, the memory of her stayed fresh. Not that I thought of her every minute, but whenever a new lady would come along I'd find myself comparing what I felt for her to what I'd felt for Camille from the first fumbling time we made love till that last hot August night we shared together—and the reality of the new was never as good as the memory of old.

Our roads had finally crossed again in New Orleans a year ago when Desire Project come to town for a concert. It was rough at first. There was a lot of old pain to get past. But now, just maybe, our separate roads might be about to merge.

Camille finally spotted me. Her eyes crinkled as she smiled. She waved and mouthed something I couldn't hear. I smiled back and waved like a simpleminded fool and tried to press a little closer to the stand. But the people ahead were packed tight. I was gonna mash me some folks if I kept pressing.

Fats had finished up at the mike with a flourish and returned to his seat. A little man with the face of a predatory bird rose to his feet and was heading to the podium, but Camille beat him to it. I couldn't have been more than thirty feet from her when she grabbed the mike.

—Ralph . . . Ralph Trapp . . . , she said, her warm, rich whisper amplified by the massive speaker system. —Come up here. I want people to meet . . .

What she was saying got interrupted by this loud cracking sound. The support for the lights and electronics suspended above the stage had snapped and given way, and a heavy mass of wires and cables and floodlights started falling toward the podium. Folks on the platform looked up at the sound, eyes widening, mouths opening, screams freezing in their throats. Then they were diving and scrambling out of the way.

For just a second, I felt relief. The heavy stuff was coming down on the chairs behind where Camille was standing. But as the debris crashed into the speaker system, Hollywood Boulevard suddenly went dark. Floodlights and streetlights and even neon signs and store windows blacked out as a short circuit, like a hole blasted in a dam, channeled current out of the main and into the grounded wires.

An electrical arc flickered brightly somewhere in the wreckage, and the cable leading to the mike in Camille's hand began to smoke and burn like an explosive fuse. I had witnessed an execution at Angola State Prison, and I knew what came next.

I started climbing over people trying to reach her, but it was like trying to swim upstream in the Mississippi during spring flood tide. The crowd that a moment before had been packed tight against the platform, trying to get close enough to bask in the warm aura of Hollywood stardom, had turned and was rushing away. It took a week to make a step, a month to go five feet.

Then the voltage hit Camille. The power arched her back, threw open her mouth, widened her eyes. As the electricity pulsed through her with incredible violence, she fell back into the rank of chairs that had just been abandoned by the Hawaiian shirt and the business suits and jeans. Still sitting upright, her hips thrusting forward, grinding back, her mouth opened wide in a soundless cry of agony.

I finally reached the stage in three or four steps over backs and shoulders and heads. As I landed on the platform, I pulled my .357, spun the chamber to a wad-cutter, and fired the round into the base of the power amp right where the mike wire connected.

It was only then, when it stopped, that I realized I'd been hearing a high whining sound since the short began. I don't know if it was the sound of electrical current—or the sound of Camille Bynum dying.

Nobody had to tell me. Shit, I've seen more death on an autumn afternoon than most doctors see in their well-padded, rich, and safe career. I lifted her off the chair and lay her gently on the unpainted boards of the platform.

A mass of shiny black curls cushioned her head. Her beautiful face was hardly marked by the years or what she'd just suffered. Her enormous dark eyes were wide open and seemed to be looking at me. But the palm of the hand that had held the mike was burned black. And the pulse and heartbeat I didn't expect to find weren't there.

Just then, some young, white street cop on traffic duty vaulted up on the platform behind me. I didn't have to look around to see that he was playing Savior of the Scene.

—Drop the gun, and lie down flat, mister, he said through his perfect teeth.

I snaked my badge case out of my coat pocket with my left hand and tossed it over my shoulder.

—If I put this gun anywhere, it's gonna be up your ass, fool, I said, and felt the tears beginning to flow down my cheeks.

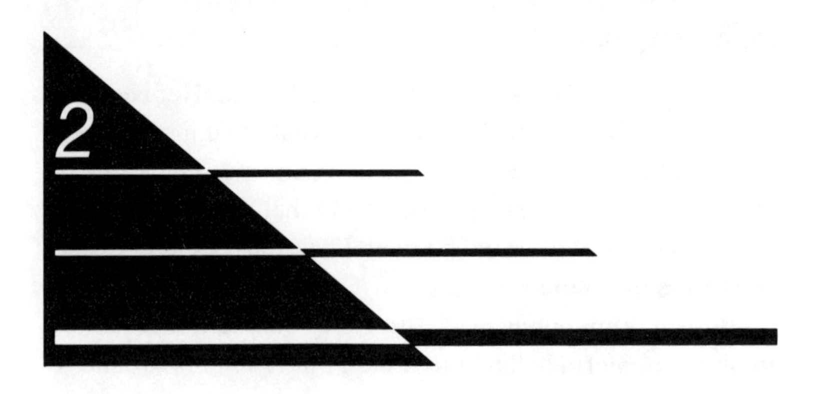

2

It was dark by the time the ambulance crew finished and took off with no siren or flashing lights. No emergency, no life to save. Just a dead woman headed for the L.A. County morgue, where they'd cut and probe and find out just exactly how Camille Bynum died. I didn't have any questions for them. I already knew.

A couple of teams from the power company were trying to get wires and lines back in order as a plainclothes detective walked over, carrying my badge. He looked like a bit player from *Dragnet,* with raw beef for a face and a suit tailored by the Volunteers of America. He didn't smile at me, and I didn't smile back.

—Captain Trapp, I'm Detective Lawrence Lonagan, L.A.P.D.

—All right.

—You saw it happen?

—Oh yeah. I didn't miss a thing.

—The officer says you discharged a weapon. . . .

—Yeah, well, see, the lady was being electrocuted. I blew out the amp.

—Los Angeles is pretty strict on discharge of firearms.

I stared at him. —Shame you weren't here. You could have bitten the 220 line in two with your teeth.

—Still, you understand, the law. . . .

I pointed over toward the Hollywood Roosevelt, where they were just getting their lights working again.

—I got a room over there. If you've got a problem, tell it to your watch chief. He'll be able to find me in the bar. For the rest of the night.

Lonagan was saying something else, like telling me he had to have my gun, but I ignored him and crossed the street. A lot of times a drink is nice. Sometimes you *got* to have one. This was sometimes.

The Cinegrill was almost empty. They had this bimbo whacking at the piano and singing these old songs. She couldn't sing, but I sure as hell didn't need to be by myself.

I was all right through a couple of quick doubles. I kept my eyes on the back bar and my ears on Cole Porter being abused by the piano. I let my mind go out and play. Anywhere it wanted, except in that old locked room with the battered door. The one that had Camille's name on it.

I knew what I was doing. I'd learned how to come up or come down a long time ago. A lot of people I'd cared about had gone on over during the years, hardly any of them from age or illness. In New Orleans, we get past it with music, drinks, and a good wake. In the army in Berlin, we'd had the drinks and vengeance on the far side of the wall. But this wasn't Berlin, and God knows it wasn't New Orleans. This was La-La Land. There was only the drinks.

I was into my third double and feeling what you might call removed when I heard a little noise, between a cough and a throat clearing. It was this short, skinny old guy. His phony smilc said he'd lied a lot, and his hand-tailored suit said he'd gotten rich doing it. For just a minute I thought he might be a funeral parlor owner come to hustle the job on Camille.

—Captain Trapp?

—Go away. I don't want none—and you sure as hell don't want none of me.

—Nat Wren, he went on, just like I'd asked him to stay a while, have a drink. He pushed an engraved card across the bar toward me.

—I don't give a fuck if you're Bobby Bluejay. Haul ass, man. I'm on this special medical regime, and I don't have no time to . . .

I stopped talking. My tongue was thick and the words were coming out like Gullah. The little man looked very sorry. He nodded like he was inside me, looking out. I thought to myself, I bet he cuts a mean deal.

—I'm a . . . I was a friend of Camille's.

Then I knew where I'd seen him before. On the platform. He was the one being introduced by the fat man, about to take the mike when Camille grabbed it.

—I did publicity for Danny and his rock group. I met Camille when she first got to California. She worked at my office from the time Danny was nine till he started Desire Project. She told me about you.

—Then you know why I'm doing my own taxidermy with Irish.

Nat Wren nodded. —My sincere condolences. Let me buy you a drink.

He waved down our waiter and spoke to him. The waiter set a bottle of Bushmills, a fresh pair of glasses, and a small pitcher of water between us. Wren poured himself a drink, looking palely earnest.

—I spoke to the investigating officer, a Detective Lonagan.

He told me something about electric leads getting plugged wrong. Then that frame collapsing and . . .

I could see that mike cable smoking and Camille jerking as the current hit her. —All right, I said shortly, stopping his recital.

—Sorry. It's just, if she hadn't taken that mike to call out to you . . .

I saw where he was going. If Camille hadn't grabbed the mike, Nat Wren would have been holding it when the current whipped through it. The pathologists would be doing a full-body check on him about now.

—Yeah, well, you were lucky.

—I feel terrible about that. And I can't help but wonder . . . Captain Trapp, Camille spoke very highly of your investigation of Danny's death. I'd feel better if you'd review the L.A.P.D. report on this . . . accident that almost killed me. Would you consider staying on in L.A. a while? At my expense, of course.

—You got any reason to think somebody's especially anxious to see you go on along?

—I've been doing PR for forty years. No matter how hard you try, people get offended. I mean, you can't make a buck out here without someone . . .

I didn't want to hear this. I wanted to see Camille to her final rest and get myself back to New Orleans, where I could lose myself in abusing miserable sonsofbitches who shot their wives or blew away a bad dope deal. I told Wren that in no uncertain terms, but he wouldn't give up.

—There's something else. A lot of my friends—old friends—have been dying lately.

I made him for his late sixties, maybe seventy.

—Nothing unusual about that, is there?

—From natural causes, no. But there's been a string of accidents. . . .

—Yeah, well, accidents happen.

Nat Wren sighed, finished off his drink.

—Yes, you're probably right. I'm being silly. This was just another terrible accident. Poor Camille . . . did she have family in New Orleans?

—Nobody's left. Except me. . . .

—If I can do anything . . .

I gestured at the bottle of Irish. —You've done it.

Nat Wren laid a bill on the bar, shook my hand, and left. I took the bottle with me to my room. A cabana with sliding glass doors that opened onto a planted terrace. In the middle was a big, blue pool with dumb-looking white commas painted on the bottom.

Wren hadn't sounded like he believed what he was saying. But then nobody much holds with chance when it deals them a bad hand. Better believe the whole world is plotting against us than admit that randomness just comes through and slaps us over on our ass. Still, if there was any chance that Camille's death wasn't an accident . . . The muscles along the back of my neck tightened.

The next day, as they say, I slept in. I think an investigator from the L.A.P.D. called about a statement, but I just said accidents happen, and hung up on him and ordered some more Irish. Later, there was another call from Wren, who said he'd handled the funeral arrangements for Camille. He'd be sending a car for me tomorrow. Then it was evening and night again, and my mind kept picking at the lock on that door with Camille's name on it. So I turned it loose inside.

Camille's momma used to have her a job with a cleaning service that tidied up the offices of brokers and lawyers in big downtown skyscrapers. After her momma left for work, Camille was alone in their project apartment. That is, till I started coming by. First I brought my school books as an excuse. Camille was smart. She helped me get through algebra. But I had a few things to teach her about biology. She'd held herself apart from those girls at Desire who gave their bodies away at twelve and started selling them at thirteen. Camille knew where that led, and she always had her mind set on another kind of life. But I wanted her more than life itself, and I wouldn't let her say no more than a hundred times. Undressing her perfect body, kissing her budding breasts, entering her became my nightly obsession. Let the other brothers rob and steal to smoke pot or ride the horse. I didn't need to. Camille was my addiction.

Our last summer was the best. I was out of school and had me a job driving a truck for a seafood dealer. I'd rush home and scrub off the smell of fish and shrimp, then head for Camille's place. We'd make love with the windows open to catch any cool breeze off Lake Pontchartrain.

Our last night together we could hear children just a little younger than us laughing and playing outside in the courtyard in the spray of an open fire hydrant. I told Camille it was time we got married, had kids of our own. Camille said she'd never want a baby of hers raised in Desire. I told her I'd saved almost two hundred dollars. We'd rent us an apartment. Maybe even one of those fancy ones with a swimming pool. I thought that would make her happy, but tears filled her eyes. I asked her how come she was crying. All she said was, she'd never learned how to swim.

Sometime before dawn, I pulled on swim trunks the hotel provided and went out to the pool and swam laps till all I could do was either drown or just manage to crawl out and fall asleep on the cement in the chill night air.

Come morning, I shaved and ordered some food from room

service. As I was finishing eating, there was a knock at the door. It was Leslie, my pretty little chauffeur. She wasn't smiling, but it was good to see a friendly face.

—Are you ready? The funeral is at eleven. Mr. Wren said he's meeting you at Forest Lawn.

Leslie drove out of Hollywood and into what they call the Valley. She said they used to raise oranges and grapefruit there. It reminded me of a cleaned-up version of Veterans Highway back in Jefferson Parish, just outside New Orleans. Mile after mile of shops and stores, plenty of dinky homes, and this funny beige-colored air that makes your eyes water, your nose cloud up, and probably causes internal bleeding.

But finally my girl made a turn and drove into this big place that looked like a cross between the world's weirdest mini-golf course and Louie's Deer Park. This was Forest Lawn.

If somebody from Hollywood tells you he knows where the bodies are buried, don't be impressed. Everybody knows. This is where they lay out the legends. If you haven't seen 'em in a movie for a while, and they don't turn up in *People* magazine anymore, this is the place.

Leslie pointed out where Valentino was staying. I wondered if he'd had it that good in life. We passed Marilyn Monroe's spot and a bunch of visitors hanging out like maybe later she'd give 'em a photo opportunity.

Finally, we come to a tent over an open plot. There were maybe thirty people sitting on party chairs or standing around. Nat Wren come over and shook my hand.

—Captain Trapp, let me introduce you to Reverend Peabody.

Reverend Peabody was white, from a church near Camille's Brentwood home, and he didn't know squat about her. She hadn't been a member of his congregation, but in a spirit of Christian charity—and for a few bills, I knew—he had come at

Nat Wren's request to deliver his all-purpose "She Will Arise" number. I nodded and sat down across from a lot of people I'd never seen before.

The expensive casket was covered with exotic tropical flowers I didn't recognize, and right next to the discreetly covered hole in the ground was Danny's headstone. It had a guitar carved into the granite, and a paraphrase of a line from one of his songs. I remembered him singing the song. I remembered the line.

Now he knows who churned the Milky Way,
who gave him night and gave him day . . .

As Reverend Peabody earned his score, my eyes drifted across the crowd of people, without any recognition. It was like Nat Wren had hired them to come mourn with me.

But then, back behind where all these strangers were sitting, I saw Lonagan leaning against a well-tended tree. If that bastard hassles me again about firing my weapon, I'm gonna be in the slam for assault, I was thinking.

Then I saw this tall guy in a dark business suit and sunshades walk up and start talking to him. Somewhere in the dead file an old, tarnished bell rang. I knew that joker. God knows from where, or why, but I knew him.

A little ways over, there were two more types in suits and dark glasses. One of them had an expensive-looking camera. The other one had a radio mike clipped to his lapel and a wire in his ear.

What the hell is going on? I wondered, feeling my shoulders stretching the fabric of my jacket. I see L.A.P.D., I see what looks like a pair of feds, I see this tall thin guy who is still ringing my bell. It looks like a mob funeral. It looks like when they put Franco Xavier Burnucci away in New Orleans. More cops than wops. It crossed my mind that maybe Camille had connections she never mentioned.

Now my eyes were moving turbo-speed, and the more I squinted and stared, the more I saw. Back at the roadside, a long black limo was parked. A sandy-haired moon-faced guy inside was talking to a fine-looking woman standing with her back to me. That goddamned bell was going off again. Something about both of 'em looked familiar, too. As I tried to place them, the guy in shades joined them and started a double-time exchange with the sandy-haired guy inside the car.

Finally, it hit me. The guy in shades was Alphonse Narbonne. Shit, I ought to know him. My momma cleaned house for his momma and saw to her when she took her time dying down at Touro Infirmary on Prytania Street. Narbonne had later turned up in Germany working for the Company when I was in a special military police unit. After one really bad operation in the wake of the Kennedy assassination that took us across the East German border, Alphonse had vanished. Dead, in the stockade, or promoted, nobody said; and in that place, those days, you didn't ask. Well, howdy, I was thinking. Here's old Al come back from the grave so he can haunt a grave. I got to find out about this.

Reverend Peabody finished up, allowing that we would all one day die, and all rise again in the arms of Jesus. I didn't especially believe it, but it seemed a nice thought on a hot, sunny October day in California. What do you expect a preacher to tell you? Dead is dead?

Nat Wren introduced me to a few people who took my hand, said they were sorry, and passed on by. One nice-looking gray-haired woman said it was a terrible thing, pressed something into my hand, and walked away with the preacher. When I looked down, I saw it was a realtor's card.

I wanted to wait till the grave was filled so I could spend a little while with the nearest thing I ever had to a family, but this fed business was still pinching the nerves in my neck, so I headed for the black limo. Anyhow, Camille and Danny had all the time in the world, and I knew I'd be back more than once.

But if I had my eye on the feds, it seems they had theirs on me—and didn't want to chat. As I reached the road, Narbonne got into the limo, and it pulled away leaving rubber. Leslie brought up the Rolls, and I jumped in beside her.

—Can you tool this thing, love-bug?

—What?

—I say, can you drive this palace?

—Sure. What do you want me to . . . ?

—See that big black stretch Lincoln?

—Uh-huh.

—Go get it.

—Like . . . follow that car?

—You got it.

—I never expected to hear that. I mean, driving a Rolls-Royce, and all . . .

She popped the sucker into low, and we left the cemetery at an undignified speed. I meant to find out what Al Narbonne was up to. He hadn't come to pay respects, and he hadn't come just for the sight of me after so many years. That tightness in my neck and shoulders wouldn't go away, and I was beginning to get the notion that maybe Nat Wren's paranoia was just good sense talking. Maybe those voices at the airport had been right to warn me about the White Zone. Too bad Camille hadn't heard them or paid them any mind.

We were zipping through streets and along avenues, but whoever was driving the Lincoln knew where the gearshift was. Leslie was doing just fine, but she couldn't seem to get us up even with the limo.

—They're heading for the Ventura Freeway, she said as if that was just the nicest thing had happened to her all day.

—That's good, huh?

—It's the pits. They must have a driver from back East.

—That could be, I said, wondering who was trying to take Narbonne out of my range.

Leslie was right. If the freeway was a traffic artery, the system was sclerotic. The Lincoln driver was better than good, swinging from one lane to another, hitting his passing gear and his brakes just right, but what can you do with a stretch limo? On the Ventura Freeway? Not one hell of a lot.

Somewhere around the Van Nuys off-ramp, he found himself between a pair of nervous Porsches and a moving van, and the whole traffic pattern was slowing to a stop.

The driver of the stretch tried a cute move. He hit the wide shoulder and gunned it. Leslie shrugged and went right behind him. He didn't get far. About fifty yards farther on, stopped on the shoulder in the broiling midday sun, was a Mercedes 280SL convertible with a fine frosted-blonde behind the wheel. She appeared to be in depth analysis with a California highway patrolman, and the CHP wasn't in any hurry to get done with her case and send her on. When he saw that Lincoln stretch boogieing on down into his consultation room, you could see the blond hair on his neck rearing up. It seems a CHP cannot abide folks trying to get one up on all the other poor bastards stuck on the freeway—especially when he's hustling one of the citizens.

—Ha. Leslie giggled as she managed to ease back into a proper traffic lane just as it came to a dead stop. —That dip just bought it. They'll skin him and burn the remains.

Sure enough, my Highwayman waved down the Lincoln and walked over to the driver's window looking a lot like Gary Cooper in *High Noon*. As he did I went out the Rolls passenger door, did my celebrated one-handed vault over the hood of a beautifully restored 1938 Oldsmobile, and tapped on the opaque side window of the limo. Highwayman never even looked at me. He was talking to the driver about his momma.

The window come down electrically, slow and smooth, and there was Al Narbonne looking like he'd just had a Hollywood breakfast of shirred shit.

—Alphonse, my man, you almost got away without speaking.

Narbonne always had a decent sense of the absurd. He shrugged at the moon-faced guy beside him, and held out a hand, smiling.

—Say, Rat. Quite a time since I saw you.

—Where you at, Narbonne? I thought the spiders across the big wall got you years ago.

—No, I lived through that. I hear you went home and got with the force.

I nodded. —What say we find a nice place with ribs and bones and beer and catch up on old times?

—Well, that sounds fine, but I got a lot to . . .

—What you got is some explaining to do. You know that was my lady they just buried.

—Oh? You knew Camille Bynum?

—Hey, Alphonse, cut the shit. I come all the way out here from New Orleans, and the best thing I've seen so far is a funeral I didn't want to go to. You know I can stay on this goddamned limo till it needs a ring job.

He turned to the sandy-haired moon-faced man and said some things. Old Sandy gave me a look and nodded.

—Okay, Al said smoothly as he scratched something on a card with one of those gold Cross ballpoint pens that costs more than a typewriter. —I'll catch you there. One o'clock. You know where Pico is?

—Don't sweat it, I said. —If Pico stays put, I'll find it.

The Highwayman was still bullshitting the driver of the limo as I walked away back toward my Rolls, which had not moved an inch during all this.

I must have been climbing back in beside Leslie when I realized that the moon-faced man with sandy hair was the Attorney General of the United States.

—Good to see you, Rat. I mean it.

No reason to reckon Narbonne didn't mean it. We had seen some rough times in Europe years before. I like to think folks who have trotted a few miles through hell together got something left over from the trip. I don't know that I believe it, but whenever I get the chance I operate like it's true—unless it's a very serious matter with no room for messing around.

We were at a little place on Pico Boulevard. As soon as I walked in, the good smells told me why Narbonne had named it. I mean, you want Southern country food in L.A., how many places can you go? I ordered the fried chicken. If they could do anything at all, they could do bird. You got to be from New Hampshire or New Jersey or some other dumb place not to do bird right.

—I'm sorry about Mrs. Bynum, Narbonne was telling me.

—That's sweet, Alphonse. Now tell me why the hell you and all those other government types just happened by the funeral. You stop in to see all U.S. citizens to their rest?

Al shrugged. —It didn't have anything to do with Camille Bynum, Rat.

—Aw, shit, man. Didn't have nothing to do with her? It was her goddamned funeral. You gonna talk to me—or are we just gonna eat chicken and bullshit each other?

—Let's eat first, Narbonne said. —We'll talk later.

They brought the chicken. Lima beans and fried okra, and hominy on the side. The corn bread was sweet and made out of real fine meal, like cake flour. That may be the way they like it in California. Back home we like coarse meal, hard-baked. But that's all right. My mind wasn't on food anyway. I watched Narbonne clean his plate, then I started in on him again.

—I want to know one thing: Was her death an accident?

Narbonne frowned and looked around like he expected all kinds of foreign enemies to be chowing down on field peas and corn bread.

—It could have been.

—But you don't think so.

Another shrug. The man used to come right at you. But a few years in Washington had laid him back. Nobody ever lost his civil service GS rating by saying too little.

—We got a lot of bodies turning up in L.A. In almost no time at all.

—What's that to you? You're still CIA, ain't you?

Al shook his head no, then gave the room another sweep with his eyes. If I hadn't wanted to hear his answer, I'd have laughed out loud.

—Secret Service, he said, as shortly as you can cough out four syllables. —Head of security for former President Reagan.

—Uh-huh. That still don't tell me why you're interested in what happened down on Hollywood Boulevard.

—We got reason to think maybe Nat Wren was supposed to have bought it.

So the little man had been right on target. Only the killer's aim hadn't. And Camille had taken the hit. I fought to keep my anger under control.

—Reckon you could tell me why you think that?

Narbonne managed to fill his mouth with most of a serving of bread pudding. He chewed and considered. Finally, he swallowed and let his voice get hard.

—Look, Trapp, you got New Orleans to think about. That's your jurisdiction. Go on home. Leave this mess to us, okay?

I forced a smile as sweet as an angel's.

—Alphonse, I'd like nothing better than to get out of this shit-eating town, but you know that's not gonna happen just yet.

—Rat, this is not old times. I mean, this isn't the goddamned Ninth Ward in New Orleans. This is . . . big. A lot of important people are mixed up in this.

—That's nice for them. And I don't give a shit. All I want to know is why the hell Camille Bynum bought herself a couple thousand amps somebody was aiming at that little old public relations whacker.

—Sure, that's all. And when you know that, you're gonna want to go right on down the line with it. I remember your tour of duty in Germany, good buddy. You never let anything go if you could move with it.

—All right.

—No, it's not all right. Because this one doesn't belong to you. This is serious. This is . . . big league.

I laid down my napkin and considered if maybe I should break old Al's jaw—just to remind him who I was. But no. I didn't have what I wanted, and a fistfight in an L.A. restaurant wasn't gonna get it for me. Narbonne was looking nervous, like he'd just as soon this family reunion of ours was over and done with. What say we change the subject, move around a little, and see where that went?

—Al, I know I'm still playing in the bushes, but do an old friend a favor. . . .

He looked like I was fixing to ask him for his gun. He didn't have to worry. Shit, I had a gun of my own.

—What?

—Back at Forest Lawn . . .

—Yeah?

—There was a woman standing beside the limo. . . .

—All right.

—I never got a good look, but I kind of thought I knew her.

—You didn't recognize her? Come on. . . .

—No, I didn't. Remember, we're talking bush league down-home boy here. . . .

—It's been ten or twelve years. But you still ought to remember, he said. —She does.

That put me on hold. I tried to scan back to my time in Germany. She had to be somebody I'd known there. But I couldn't pick her out of the deep, twisted underbrush of the past.

—Candace Prescott, Al said in a flat voice, and a whole section of the past snapped into focus.

Sure enough. Candy, with the California tan and the long straight hair. She was very young, only a year or so out of college. You could see her on a war protest march easier than working in the embassy basement as a Company code clerk. Vietnam was hardly over, and CIA recruitment among the college crowd was at an all-time low. I'd told myself I just had to find out why she'd picked decoding in Berlin over sunbathing in Malibu. Can't say we ever got around to talking about that, though.

—Yeah, well now. I guess I do remember her.

—You ought to. She cost you a future. You were wasted in the army. You could've been a Company sector chief in charge of a continent by now.

I couldn't help grinning. —Who needs a continent? Anyhow, it was worth it, Alphonse.

—They told you not to go after her. A direct military order.

—Yeah, I guess I misinterpreted. I thought they were saying for me not to go and get caught.

Al laughed and shook his head. I went to remembering.

I was walking along a cold, dark hallway in the Friedrichsheim section of East Berlin. The floor groaned under my weight, and I tried to stay on the edge of the worn carpet runner, off the cracked floorboards beneath it. The silenced semiautomatic I was carrying seemed to get heavier as I walked on. I had to keep my shaky finger outside the trigger guard, or I was gonna waste the walls.

I stopped outside a door where weak light was filling a crack at the bottom. From inside, I could hear a radio playing softly. It was old-time American jazz. Bunk Johnson or Papa Celestine. Cranky horns, flat beat like somebody dropping auto batteries on the floor one after another. A clarinet noodling around over it all like a starling curving, dancing, above an old oak. "Just a Closer Walk with Thee." God Almighty, that sure fit the situation.

I pulled the pin from a canister, laid it down quick outside the door, and got myself as far away as I could in a long three count. Then I heard this loud booming sound like somebody blew their speakers, turning the Moody Blues up just a tad too high. I was back down the hallway before the reverbs stopped.

I didn't even have to kick the door down. It was already swinging on its hinges and some silly-looking blond bastard was rolling on the floor with both hands over his ears. I eased his pain with a spurt from the silenced semi, and turned to stitch another clown who thought he could draw and fire with blood running out of his ears. When those sweet 9mm slugs ran up from his crotch to his throat, he looked downright surprised and fell backward into what was left of the fireplace. I lost a second watching the smoldering embers catch his coat afire.

Then the door from the other room opened, and this baldheaded Russian dude with thick red eyebrows stepped through, hands in the air. I swear to God, he was smiling. I almost stamped his passport, too, but he motioned behind him, and Candace stepped into the room. She couldn't hear too well, but all her major parts seemed to be in place. She was shaking her head and crying, but that was nothing. If I'd been ten or twelve feet from a C-67 concussion grenade, I'd have been sniveling a little myself.

—Listen, the baldheaded man was saying, —this was a mistake. We didn't know. We thought she was Operations. We took a goddamned code clerk. . . .

I nodded at him. —All right. What are you gonna do about it?

—It's my mistake, he told me. —I'll see to it. Take the woman and walk away.

Candy was leaning on a chair retching. Code clerks don't see too many people blown to hell.

I tended to believe the baldheaded guy. He didn't look scared, like he was trying to save his Slavic KGB ass.

—If you let us walk away, how are you gonna write this up?

—Nothing easier. I command Blue Section. I write it up however I want.

I pushed Candy toward the hall. We were halfway out the hall door when Baldie spoke again.

—One thing . . .

—Yeah?

—Why did you come for her? Why is she valuable?

I stopped in my tracks and looked Candy over—dark, fright-

ened eyes, hair the color of Damascus steel, a body an artist would kill to paint, to sculpt—hell, just to touch.

—Shit, man, I called back to the Russian, —if you can't figure that out, you guys have already lost everything that matters.

As we started down the dim, shabby stairway for the street, for an old Citroën that would carry us to Checkpoint Charlie in less time than it would take Baldie to change his mind, I heard him laughing up there. Standing there, over the bodies of his men, laughing like I'd told him the best goddamned story he'd heard in a long, long time.

—Did Candy see me, I asked?

—Oh yeah. She lost her voice, got it back, then hitched a ride away from there with Lonagan.

—Seems like she could have hung around and passed the time of day—like you did.

Al laughed. —You motherfucker. I should have known you'd drive us into the ground.

—Candy's still CIA?

—Never left. Did codes, did counterespionage, then joined the Operations directorate.

—Jesus, she just don't learn, does she?

Al shrugged another time. —Some people take pride in serving their country, he said stiffly.

—Will there be a problem if I look up a lady I once did a favor for?

—Better not. She's having trouble. Some people wonder about her reliability.

—They sure didn't wonder when she was over East. They expected her to go on down with her legs crossed and her mouth shut.

—Huh, Alphonse muttered. —Those bastards didn't care

about her legs. They just wanted to sew her face closed. Anyhow, man, that was a dozen years ago. This is now.

—You want to tell me how come they're wondering about her?

Narbonne shook his head like he hadn't slept in a week. Then he wrote something on a card and handed it to me.

—You can find her here. She'll tell you if she wants to.

—She'll want to.

—Sure she will. You're good with women in trouble.

—Women are always in trouble.

Al laughed and slapped the table. —Sure. 'Cause of men like you.

I looked at the card. It was an address and phone number for a bookshop on Fairfax. I smiled at Al and grabbed the check when it came.

—Now, you ready to tell me about this mess that Camille got caught up in?

—Man, you never let go wringing and twisting till the last drop falls. If you go to fucking me over on this, I'll see you in the federal penitentiary, he almost whispered.

He was serious, but he looked like he wanted to talk about it, like whatever it was had been addling his brains, like he could use a second opinion.

—Come on, Alphonse, when did I ever fuck you over?

—All right. Your little buddy, Nat Wren . . .

—He was Camille's friend, not mine.

—If he'd bought it, he would have fit a pattern we've noticed.

—What pattern?

—The Service computer's programmed to find certain patterns, he said slowly. —It kicked out the info on four old men who died funny in Southern California in the past six weeks. Maybe they were accidents, maybe not. But we're sniffing around.

—What the hell's four old men got to do with the Secret Service? I asked him.

He smiled, but there wasn't any humor in his voice when he answered my question.

—One common element among them. They were all old and close friends of former President Reagan.

I let Leslie drop me at the Fairfax address and go on. It was nothing but a storefront and a deep, narrow shop behind that seemed to go back to a vanishing point in the rear. MILTON HEBRON, JUDAICA AND RARE BOOKS, the sign said. Watching that Rolls slide away, I wondered if I'd sent the car off too soon. I had no idea what the place might have to do with Candace Prescott.

But I was sure Narbonne wasn't jerking me around. That would be dumb, and he wasn't. I entered and heard a bell announce to someone I was on the territory. My eyes adjusted to the dim light as I looked around.

Bookshelves stretched back and up, each one packed solid with old books in more languages than I could make out. Hand-printed signs identified the Judaica section right next to one on Socialist thought, followed by one filled with works on Progressivism, the Industrial Workers of the World, the American Worker's Party, trade unions—a lot of stuff I'd never had time for.

A woman, with her back to me, was stacking Xeroxed copies of a paper called *The Loyalist* on a display table that already held untidy piles of *The Jewish Forward, Masses,* and *The Daily Worker.* I sort of cleared my throat, and she turned to look at me with no sign of greeting in her eyes. The woman was ancient, but dressed with style like she was still a player. She had the hard-surface glitter of a female who was making it in man's world thirty years before Betty Friedan got her consciousness kicked up. I'd bet a hundred bucks American that she was from New York.

Since she was the only one in the shop, I almost spoke to her, but she turned away as a little man pushing seventy come through a door at the rear. He had soft brown eyes and a rim of curly gray hair still left from his younger days, and was dressed in baggy brown pants and a beige shirt that looked like somebody had smoked a stogie through it. His smile said he'd seen a lot of shit in his time, but he'd found a way not to let it trouble him too much.

He held an envelope out to the woman. —Here're the September receipts, Carole. Not many sales of *The Loyalist* last month, I'm afraid.

The woman didn't bother to glance in the envelope before she stuffed it into a large leather satchel she carried jammed to overflowing with papers. Money didn't seem to interest her much.

—When can I expect your article on the New Fascism, Milt? she said to the old man. —I want it for next month's lead story. I have a deadline to meet, you know.

Her tone was unpleasant and a little shrill, like a wife nagging a derelict husband. The old man promised he would work on it, and eased her toward the door to the street.

But she wasn't to be got rid of so easily. As they stood talking in quiet tones that didn't carry to me, I took down a nice volume bound in red buckram, part of a set. I opened it up to see what it was in there I didn't know. "When R. Johanan finished the

Book of Job, he used to say the following: 'The end of man is to die, and the end of a beast is to be slaughtered, and all are doomed to die. . . .' " Well, shit, I already pretty much knew that.

—The Soncino Press edition of the Talmud, the man's soft voice said behind me. —The very best English translation. I can make you a good price on it.

—No, thanks, I said. —Just browsing till you got done with your customer.

He smiled at that. —Sorry to be so long. Carole's an old friend. What can I help you with?

—Al Narbonne said I could find Candace Prescott here. I'm Ralph Trapp.

He smiled some more and offered me his hand.

—Milton Hebron. I didn't think you looked Jewish, he said, and then paused. —But I know that name. When I hear that name, it makes me remember good things. How do I know your name?

—Candy and I worked together. In Germany. A dozen years or so ago.

—Rat, he said suddenly, slapping his thigh, those eyes lighting up. —You're Rat Trapp.

—That's a fact.

—I owe you my daughter's life. How am I supposed to thank you for that?

I guess I looked surprised. Candy hadn't said anything about her folks, but I never expected a Jewish bookseller named Hebron to turn up.

—No thanks called for, I said. —We needed each other over there. It was hard going.

Hebron nodded. —They sent her home right afterward. It took her a while to settle inside. Every time she heard a loud noise . . .

—Yeah, well, we got like that if we stayed at it long. Noises—or no noise at all. A car door slamming when you didn't expect it. Birds flying out of the trees when they ought to stay put. Every little change was a message.

—I know. Once, a long time ago, I went through that.

—Second World War?

He shook his head, smiled. —No. They wouldn't let me fight in that one.

—Wouldn't let you?

—I'd fought . . . for the Loyalists in Spain.

I looked blank. That didn't mean much to me. I don't keep a logbook of wars in my head.

Milton Hebron smiled depreciatingly. —You're still a young man. You weren't even born. How would you know? Anyhow, if you'd fought for the Loyalists in 1937 and '38, maybe they didn't let you fight for America in 1942.

—I thought back then they were drafting anything that moved. Unless you were blind, deaf, flat-footed . . .

—Or fought with the International Brigade.

That name rang a bell. What do you know? Here's my Candy's dad, an old-time Red. Which made it even stranger she'd ended up working with the Company.

The old man beckoned me to the rear of the store. Behind a door marked private, he had himself a nice place. I wondered why he bothered with the door since his living space was just like the front: packed with books, piles of them on tables and in chairs. Books on the window ledges, heaped up against the wall wherever there was room. Something soft and classical was playing on a new CD machine—the only thing in the room that looked like it dated past 1940.

Hebron found a bottle and set it down on a table between two disintegrating old leather chairs. Then he got out two coffee cups and filled them with El Presidente brandy.

Funny how tired and dry you can get at funerals. I looked out the big back window that opened up onto a sandy courtyard filled with low, bushy evergreens, something that looked like a lemon tree, a line of potted cactuses, and thick-leafed jade plants—and that rich late-afternoon California sun that looks so warm in a Technicolor print.

—Candy never said much about her daddy.

He touched his cup to mine and threw the brandy down like a pro. Then he grinned like something didn't matter even though it did.

—Her mother and I separated long ago. Elaine raised Candace. She chooses to use her mother's name.

He poured us more of that sweet Mexican brandy, and I got the feeling that Milton Hebron did a lot of drinking while he read.

—So what brings you to California—if it's all right to ask. I never know with Candace's friends.

—I'm just a cop now, with no state secrets. I came to see a lady I used to know. I stayed for her funeral.

He asked, so I told him what had happened. When I mentioned Nat Wren, the muscles in his jaw twisted and just for a minute Milton Hebron didn't look like a kindly little old bookseller anymore. His eyes went hard, and he had trouble getting his mouth under control. I wondered just what kind of soldier he'd been in Spain all those years ago. He whispered something under his breath in some language I didn't know. I only understood one word.

— . . . Wren . . .

He made it sound like a curse or a warning. It wasn't anywhere mean enough to light my fire, but at least I knew where some of that bad blood Nat Wren worried about had flowed to ground. Then, just as quickly, my kindly old bookseller was smiling again. I liked how quick he could pull things together, but I was glad he didn't feel that way about me, never mind seventy and half my size.

—I'm sorry, Mr. Trapp. Sometimes we remember things too long, eh?

I was about to say, That depends on how deep the wound goes or how fine the love was. I'd remembered Camille for twenty years. I doubted I was going to forget her in twenty more. But as I opened my mouth I heard that little shop bell tinkle, and knew there was someone out in the store.

Hebron's eyes darted toward the door, and he half rose to his feet as if maybe this visitor wasn't friendly. Then his face relaxed as he saw who was entering.

—It's Candace, he said.

She came in wearing a light beige suit, carrying a fine-looking camel's-hair coat over her arm. She stopped as I got up to greet her. They say some women can beat Time in an eighty-year dash from a standing start. Candace Prescott had a lot of years yet to run, but in her mid-thirties she was way out ahead already.

I found myself looking for signs, marks—something that would prove we hadn't seen each other in over a dozen years. That wonderful hair, dark as a gun barrel, was shorter but hadn't lost its luster. Her eyes were still smoldering, her skin smooth and lightly tanned. Women's suits don't advertise their bodies unless the body is out of sight. Candy's was, and the soft beige cloth surrendered and followed the flow of her breasts and hips and thighs as if it had been applied molten and still held the heat of its fitting.

—Hello, Rat, she said with no surprise in her tone.

—Candy, I answered, wishing I'd cleared my throat first.

Her lips were cool as she brushed them against my cheek, but the way she brought her body close to mine rang bells I'd thought were broken up and sent to the foundry a dozen years ago.

Then, as quickly, I saw her eyes go past me to her father. She pulled back and threw her coat on a sofa covered with books.

—Al told me he'd had lunch with you. I see you've met . . . my father.

—Yeah. We were talking about old times.

That caught her attention for a moment. Her eyes were suddenly as chill as Hebron's had been at the mention of Nat Wren.

—You shouldn't bore your guests with ancient history, Daddy.

Milton Hebron picked up on the weather as quickly as I did. He gave the best smile he had in stock and came up out of his chair.

—I'll shut the store, he said absently. —It's almost sundown . . . Shabbot . . .

I watched Candy watching him pass. For a moment, the place was a small hotel called the Goldenes Kreuz, just off the Bahnhofstrasse, and we were young and in Europe and playing the most dangerous blood sport anybody had ever thought up. I was trying to tell her she was a fool, that only fools volunteer to be a decoy. But she was young and inexperienced and seemed to think she was going to live forever, win every round, and be assumed into Glory alive and unmarked one bright morning with some choir singing "America the Beautiful" on the sound track. Only it had gone down like I said it would. Jacobs in Blue Section had gone for the bait like a frog after a Junie bug, and I had to go in against orders and pull Candy back from the edge of eternity. She'd been sent home for R&R, and I'd been given my discharge papers.

When she turned back, her eyes met mine for a long moment. I believe they were damp.

—I'm so sorry about this afternoon. . . .

Maybe she was. It would take me a little while to fine-tune, to readjust my built-in shit-detector to her frequency.

—Al told you. . . .

—Al had a lot to say.

She glanced toward the door to the shop.

—Listen, she said in a clipped, breathless whisper, —for God's sake don't say anything in front of him. Nothing about anything you didn't read in the newspapers this year.

Just then, Milton Hebron shuffled back in, smile in place, hands in the pockets of his baggy trousers.

—A little supper now, he said. —A little celebration . . .

When supper was done, Candy and I said good-bye to her father and walked out into the California night together. I understood why the natives carry a good coat. There's something to those old song lyrics: "Hate California, it's cold and it's damp. . . ." If you thought you were hot when the sun was high, just hang in. When the sun goes down, you're gonna wish it was back.

—I thought you were staying here, I said.

—No, I'm at my mother's. You have a car?

—Just for the funeral. I sent it away.

—Then I'll drive you to your hotel.

—I can get a cab.

—Get a cab in L.A.? Don't even think about it. Anyhow, don't we have things to say?

Nothing personal had come up during the meal. Hebron had started with some prayers, a glass of wine all around, good food, and some more wine. He'd been a little drunk by then, and there'd been talk of the old days in Brooklyn when he was a boy, talk of losing his religion, trying to piece out the emptiness with Leftist politics, then, in latter days, finding Judaism once more like a lost love whose name you barely remembered, whose voice you could never forget.

It was good after-dinner talk, and I knew the changes he was ringing his way through. I hadn't been to Mass in a lot of years, but you never know. When the last red-rimmed sun goes down and a hard, freezing rain starts to fall, I might find myself outside St. Louis Cathedral across from Jackson Square. And I might go in. I don't remember slamming the door when I left.

So yes, Candy and I still had things to say. If not then, when?

She was driving a white BMW that hummed like it was on batteries. She said it belonged to her mother. We drove up Fairfax to Hollywood Boulevard, then down to the Roosevelt.

We passed the spot near the Chinese Theatre, where a few days before a crowd had been gathered to see a new star for Danny Bynum unveiled. Some tourists were taking photos of the red granite star with the brass record and Danny's name inset in it. I wondered if they knew or cared it marked the spot where Camille had died.

I tried to lead Candy to my room, but she stopped on the patio outside and settled into one of the white metal lounge chairs that circled the big lighted pool. I complained. It was too damned cold for normal people to be outside that night.

—Quit complaining, Candy said. —It was colder than this on the Unter den Linden. I never heard you gripe. You just dropped a jigger of schnapps into a liter of beer and kept right on trucking.

I laughed and remembered. —I was younger, tougher. I was conditioned—and I had on army underwear.

Candy raised an eyebrow. —No you didn't, she reminded me. —You didn't have on any underwear at all.

—Bite your tongue, girl. You'll ruin my reputation.

She giggled. I smiled back, but the thought was passing through my mind that it should be Camille and me here now sharing memories.

—You're still a long way off, Candy said softly.

—You know why, I said. —You were at Forest Lawn this morning.

Candy dropped her eyes.

—Camille Bynum was the one, wasn't she? Why you and I never quite . . .

—Oh, baby, have you forgot? We did. We did, a whole lot, every chance we got.

— . . . got permanent.

—Well, now, that's a whole 'nother thing. Maybe I figured that a roll in the hay in Europe was one thing, but a nice girl like you wouldn't want to spend the rest of her life explaining this great big black guy following her around.

—That's a damned lie and you know it, she said hotly.

I reached over and touched her hand in apology.

—You're right. It is. And she was. I never got past Camille. Lord knows I tried. I'd get even, fall back, push ahead. . . . But I couldn't get past the picture of us back together one day. Not the idea. Lord knows, not the belief. Just that goddamned picture. . . .

Candace smiled and put her hand on mine.

—That makes it a little better. When the Company finally let me go back to Germany, people we knew there told me you'd left the army and gone back home. I always wondered why you didn't wait for me. Ask me to . . . drop out of the Company and go find out if I liked New Orleans. I thought it was something wrong with me, something I lacked.

Jesus, the pain we give and get with no one intending it.

—I guess I should have told you early on about Camille. We grew up together, you see. . . .

—I know all about her now. Camille Bynum. Born New Orleans, 1946. Never married, one son who predeceased her. Only known sensitive connections to the Burnucci family in New Orleans.

She looked at me, suddenly thoughtful, her eyes cool, detached from any emotion that had passed between us.

—Any chance the Burnucci people took down Camille Bynum? she asked.

—No. She . . . severed that connection about a year ago. All the Burnuccis she knew are dead.

Candy nodded, looking glum.

—So it had to be Nat Wren they were going for.

—That's what Al Narbonne and all his clever folks think.

—Al told you what's going down?

—Come on, Candy. You know better. He put a lot of nervous little shit on me like all those Washington blowflies spread around.

She shrugged like Al. It seemed there was some kind of nervous ailment going around among the government types and Candy had caught it. I guess twelve years' exposure sort of guaranteed she would have.

—This thing could cost me my career.

I just gave her this look of mild surprise.

—Career? You give a shit about that? I never understood why you went with the Company to begin with.

Candy looked away at the blue pool a long minute before answering. A chill breeze cut through the palm trees and ruffled her hair.

—I guess I was trying to prove something.

—What the hell does that mean?

—My father . . . He's been sensitive since before I was born.

—Why? That goddamned Spanish War business?

—He told you about that?

—I told you we talked about old times. Didn't a lot of people go fight in Spain?

She nodded. —Some. People with big splashy egos and the political intelligence of three-toed sloths. It was a lousy war with nothing but sonsofbitches on both sides. To pick a side, you had to be stupid.

I had the feeling she was talking about her father, how she

felt about him. Never mind the Spanish War or what happened over there. Just him.

—Girl, we're talking fifty years ago. What does anybody care?

She looked weary, as if all those years had come to roost on her shoulders.

—If he'd let it go, people up high might have forgotten by now. But he's never regretted it. He still contributes articles to *The Loyalist*—and Carole Klein, his close friend and the publisher of that paper, is a stone Stalinist. Some say she may even be a sleeper working for the faction that's resisting Gorbachev.

I must have looked stoned myself. That nagging woman I'd seen at the bookstore a sleeper? If she was part of a spy apparatus, I was a model for *Vogue*. I'd dealt with the FBI, the CIA, the DEA, and half a dozen others. I knew those cretins in the agencies with all the letters for names were playing poker with pinochle decks, but this was the wildest yet.

—So then why are you here? Wait. Let me guess. To use your father to uncover Hollywood Reds who don't like *glasnost* and *perestroika*—and might be killing Reagan's old card-playing buddies to create an incident? Right?

She nodded with this troubled look I remembered from a long time ago.

—Ridiculous, I said.

—Rat, there's proof that . . . No, I can't tell you any more. I really can't.

She pulled her camel's-hair coat around her and rose to her feet in a quick, easy motion. —I have to go now. My mother's expecting me. She invited some people over I haven't seen in years.

I grabbed her arm. —Just tell me one thing. Is there any proof what happened on Hollywood Boulevard wasn't an accident? That Camille was murdered?

—Not really. We think that accident was arranged. That they

were after Nat Wren, because his name belongs on the list of old friends of former President Reagan. But we're not sure.

—Al said there'd been four other deaths. I want the names.

She paused a moment, her dark eyes fixed on mine. Then answered in a low voice. —Harold Swanson, Louis Werner, Will Mohr, and Abe Peretz.

—Has anyone questioned Wren about those guys?

—No, the investigation has been conducted very privately.

—It's about to go public.

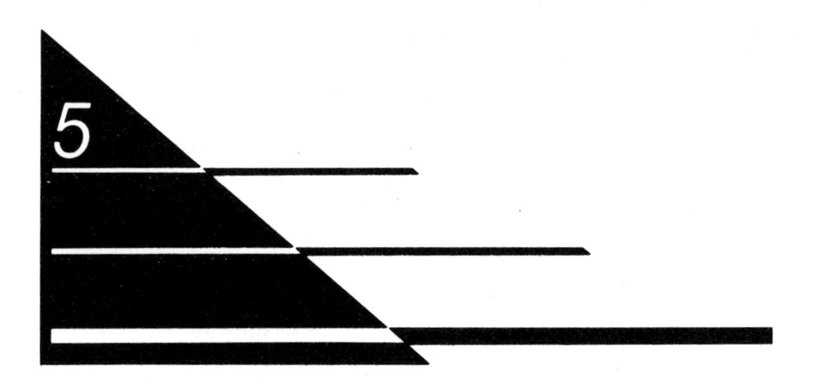

I fished among the hotel stationery in the desk drawer, looking for Nat Wren's card. Sure enough, it had a home phone number on it. I dialed and listened as an answering machine played me back Wren's voice.

—This is Nat Wren. Leave a message at the tone and I'll get back to you. If this is Harry, I'll see you tonight at Athena's.

Shit. If this was New Orleans I'd have connections who'd tell me in fifteen minutes Athena's last name, her address, and what was going on between her and Wren. Here the best I had was a phone directory with ten million names in it. Fat chance of finding Wren before he got ready to come home—if he came home tonight.

I decided to order a bottle of Irish to keep me company while I waited. I had opened the desk drawer to find the card that tells you what number to dial for room service, before it suddenly hit me that Athena just might be a what instead of a who. I dialed the hotel operator.

—Can you check the address of a restaurant named Athena's?

This low familiar chuckle come back at me. —No need. It

happens to be a favorite of mine. It's in West Hollywood. On Melrose, near Doheney. Will you need a cab?

It took less than twenty minutes to get there—ten of them waiting for the station wagon taxi to come lumbering up to the Roosevelt. The driver looked crushed I wasn't headed for LAX. Even the damned cabbies wanted me to leave town.

Athena's was a big bar with a small restaurant attached. It had fake Grecian pillars out front and very strange critters inside. So that's why the hotel operator gave me that confidential snicker.

Queer bars are nothing out of the ordinary if you work New Orleans, but this one was different. Maybe the folks who break loose from reality have more imagination in California. If Athena's was typical, they sure as hell have more money. Lots of velvet and satin, leather and gold leaf. I'm not gonna talk about the murals on the walls. I hear Greeks pulled a lot of strange shit when they weren't putting together geometry and logic, but I got to believe the boys that did Athena's were making stuff up.

There were guys in leather, guys in silk shirts, big guys and little ones, white and black and a few shades you don't see much of in the deep South. I looked behind the bar to see if I could spot who was making the money off these bums. There he was. Maybe forty, bald, dressed in a tie-dyed mauve shirt. With taste like that, he had to run the place.

—I'm looking for Nat Wren, I mentioned to him across the bar.

His eyebrows did a number like the arch at St. Louis.

—Well, he never told *me* he was waiting for a big good-looking . . .

—Listen, motherfucker, I said with a certain intimate suggestiveness. —You say where Wren is, or I'll tear off your action and feed it to that potted meat down at the end of the bar.

Even in semidarkness, he looked suddenly pale.

—Nat left.

—Which way?

—Out the back. There's a parking lot . . .

—How long ago?

—Not long. Listen, he'll probably be right back. He was looking for Harry when he came in. Then someone started talking to him and . . . you know. His car's out back and . . . Your first drink is on the house if you want to wait.

I didn't. I turned away and started toward the rear of the place—to coin a phrase. Then I realized this big, ugly dark-complexioned sonofabitch sitting at the end of the bar was looking me over. He was dressed in a velvet smoking jacket with a cigarillo in his hand and a glass of red wine on the bar in front of him. He did a little take with his shoulders.

—You are so . . . *big*, he said with what I reckon he meant to be a friendly smile.

I ignored him and tried to get past him, but old Smoking Jacket got off his bar stool and kind of loomed up in front of me. You know what? That sonofabitch was four inches taller than me, and maybe forty pounds more meat on him, too. Oh hell, here I am, looking for Wren, and I've done flushed the biggest queer on the West Coast.

—What do you like? he asked me.

—You wouldn't believe what I like, I told him, and tried to edge away.

—I like *you*. We need to talk. . . .

No we didn't. Time was dripping away like blood while I was messing with this critter instead of finding Nat Wren.

—I'm coming through, old son. You want to move?

—I think you're *wonderful*, he said and reached for me with the biggest pair of hands I'd ever seen.

Goddammit to hell, I thought, am I gonna have to kill this big sissy to get clear? I believe I am.

I had pulled my piece once since I got to this shit-eating town, and there'd been a cop on my case in a Shreveport second. Now I was gonna have to do it again—and you wanna bet there'd be five queer cops wanting to take me in for threatening harm to an inoffensive citizen who just wanted to check my package?

Never mind. First things first. I laid my .357 on my man's sternum and gave him smile for smile.

—You want to take a long pull on this, Geronimo? I asked him.

You'd have thought I mentioned his momma. In fact, I got the feeling everybody in Athena's thought I was just plain crude. That hurt, but on the other hand I was down the hallway and out into the alley in back five seconds later.

That's when the first surprise hit me. It had started raining. Colder than ever and a thin European kind of mist falling. The alley was narrow and high, with garbage cans and a dumpster and some sawhorses and all the junk you expect outside a business. Down at the end, it looked like a high, blank, white stucco wall. But what seemed to be a cul-de-sac was just a sharp right-hand turn out of the alley into a parking area. As I neared that turn I heard a scream.

Not any kind of scream. Not what you hear when the family mutt nails the postman. Not even what I've heard in a fire fight when a man finds out he just took one in the gut. Worse. The kind of scream that comes out of a man when he's facing that most terrible nightmare that's been dogging him forever, the one that's been running just behind him and, after so long, finally caught up. It came again and again, and I broke into a flat-out run. I wanted to see what that nightmare looked like, and who was dreaming in the rain, in L.A.

But somebody was waiting for me at the end of the alley, and a blow from something hard and metallic caught me in the side of my head and sent me sprawling. My last thought was that my suit would only be good for a Salvation Army dumpster after sliding across that wet greasy pavement.

It had to be a few minutes before I come to. And a couple more before I cleared the cobwebs from my brain. As I regained my feet, all I was sure of was I heard only silence. The screaming had stopped.

In the parking lot, flaring yellow sodium streetlights reflected off dark, shining asphalt. A handful of cars were scattered here and there. I took out my Magnum, but there was nothing to see but a garbage dumpster set on rotting wood and the rain drifting down into it and the rest of the parking lot. Nothing, nobody.

I was about to holster my piece when I heard something, a sound like water gurgling, from the dumpster. Probably the collecting rain displacing the garbage inside. I climbed up on the side anyhow and looked in. I was wrong about the rain. Somebody had turned Nat Wren into garbage.

He was sprawled on plastic sacks full of coffee grounds and fish bones, his eyes staring up at the sodium lights, unblinking in the rain. His pants had been pulled down and somebody with the skills of a crazy surgeon had done a job of work on him. His belly was cut open, intestines running down into the orange skins and milk cartons below. They had hacked off his action, and left it stuffed into his mouth. I couldn't tell if he was dead or alive, but it would only matter for a moment or two. The paper and trash below were awash in blood and rain.

I climbed back down and leaned against the cold metal of the dumpster feeling sick and washed out. It was meant to look like queer bashing, but I knew better. Candy and the ABC agencies were right about their list. And Camille had been killed. Not because anybody wanted her dead, but because she stepped forward to welcome me to the White Zone just as Nat Wren was reaching for that microphone.

From the corner of my eye, I saw movement out in the parking lot. It was a big black stretch limo pulling out of a parking place between a beat-up van and one of those pickups with monster tires and suspension.

—Hey, I yelled as the limo headed for me. —Hey, you bastards, stop, police . . .

It was picking up speed as I leveled my pistol. In New Orleans, I'd have let go and given the driver a third eye. Easy shot. But this wasn't my town. What if I popped the chauffeur of a super-rich L.A. faggot who'd just tiptoed away from Athena's? Bad idea. No need to get stuck up in bureaucracy. I had this sucker made. Unless he had in mind to drive to Japan overnight, I'd find him.

So I jumped back to the side of the dumpster and let the limo barrel on by. But as it did, and before I scratched down its license in my mind, a face stared out of an open window at me, a face I knew—a face out of the past like Narbonne's or Candy's. Bright blue eyes, bald-shaven head, thick red eyebrows, and something almost like a smile on its lips. But not quite.

The limo screeched and chattered away then, fishtailing as it reached Melrose Avenue and headed west. The license was easy to remember. Only a couple of letters and a number. A diplomatic plate no doubt. And that meant the guy inside might have a license to kill.

The rain had tapered off, and L.A.P.D. was all over the place like lint on a cheap suit. They'd flushed out the collective weirdness from Athena's and questioned them till they started hissing about civil rights violations and threatening big scary law suits, but the bottom line was the cops couldn't make much of anything in the way of connections.

Sure, everybody knew Nat Wren—only he called himself Big Bird around Athena's. He had money, and sometimes he bought action. But if anybody had been involved in the Bird's last flight, you sure couldn't prove it by the feathers on anybody's lips.

The street bulls were pressing me. Then the plainclothes people started in. Serious hard eyes, nasty talk. I just shucked and jived and laughed and did old police-buddy business and told them there wasn't gonna be no communication of any kind whatever till I saw Mr. Narbonne of the U.S. Secret Service.

—What's the Secret Service got to do with an L.A. homicide, brother? this black detective almost as big as me started in.

—Not a thing, bruh, I told him. —Except I got nothing for you till I've seen the man.

We went through the whole scene three or four times as the M.E. and Forensics got done with what they do. Nat Wren's body had been hoisted out of the dumpster, more or less reconstituted in proper order, and dropped in a body bag on his way to Forest Lawn—by way of the county morgue where the pathologist was gonna finish what Nat's antagonists had begun—before the L.A.P.D. finally got the drift and put in a call for Narbonne.

Narbonne showed up looking rumpled and tired. I got the feeling he wasn't ready to do a thing for me.

—What is this, Trapp? I told you to lay off and you . . .

—Yeah, well, see, I wanted to ask Wren about Swanson, Werner, Mohr, and Peretz.

—Oh, for God's sake. Who told you those . . . ? Candace, of course.

—Just the names. Nothing more. I was gonna ask Wren about 'em. Now you're gonna have to let me in the game, tell me who the players are.

Al Narbonne wasn't happy, but I think he liked it that I wasn't laughing up my sleeve at him anymore.

—We know how to do our job without your help, he said stiffly.

—Tell it to Lincoln, Garfield, McKinley, and Kennedy, I laughed.

He didn't think it was funny.

—Okay, I'm telling you again. This isn't your jurisdiction. I don't want to hear about you talking to any more people.

—What about the limo? The police get anything on that?

—It's a diplomatic plate, all right. Soviet Consulate.

That was no surprise. —Guess who's fooling around L.A.? I asked Narbonne.

—Who?

—Jacobs. Blue Section, KGB.

Narbonne recognized the name. Hell, if you ever shook out the wastebaskets and mopped the floor at any Western intelligence center, you knew Jacobs and Blue Section.

—Jesus. Jesus Christ . . . so it is a KGB operation?

—Yeah, well, I can see how Jacobs being here might affect your thinking since you were already thinking that way before he showed up.

—I need you, he started. I cut him off.

—Need me? Bite your tongue, Narbonne. I got to get back to N'awlins. Cotton to make, catfish to catch . . .

He shook his head like he couldn't believe what he thought he knew for sure.

—You're the only person I know who's ever seen Jacobs. They must have him buried under deep cover at the Soviet consulate. Probably got him down as an expert in yellow-fin tuna breeding. But we've got to find him and stop these killings.

—Well, good luck, I told him. —I got bags to pack.

—Wait . . .

—Bullshit. You hung me up waiting since I had to run you down to say Hi.

—Rat, I want a description.

—Alphonse, I wouldn't piss in your ear if your brains was on fire.

—I can let L.A. book you on that .357 you like to carry. By the time it goes through channels, you'll be pushing retirement.

—Yeah, and when I'm drawing my pension, you'll still be wondering what Jacobs looks like.

We went around a couple more turns, and then Narbonne decided he was gonna have to cut me in, let me play with him. But, he said, first he'd have to make some phone calls. I told him to make the last to New Orleans, requesting me for detached duty with the Secret Service. I knew Major Mauvais would shake his head, wonder what presidential security was coming to—and say sure.

—We've got a file with pictures of everybody at the Russian consulate, Narbonne was saying.

—Reckon I can start in on that tomorrow morning after you make those calls, I told him.

Narbonne didn't look happy, but he nodded and cut out.

The black detective named Henry Harleaux decided I wasn't being a bad ass, and offered to give me a lift home.

I told him I wasn't ready to call it a night yet and pulled out the address Candy had given me before she left.

—Do you know where Seventeen Bellagio Terrace is?

He looked surprised. —You got friends in Bel Air? he asked.

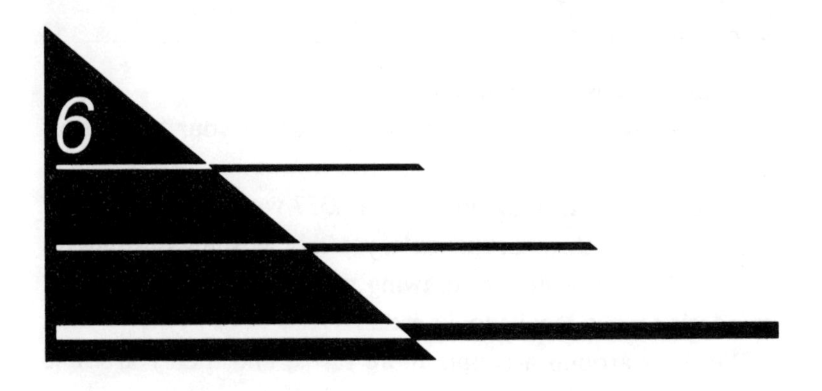

—You know a lot of folks out here? Harleaux asked me as we drove out Sunset Boulevard. The misty rain had stopped, but the street was still damp and a light fog reflected the car's headlights back at us.

—I didn't think I knew anybody out here, I told him. —But I met this woman I knew a long time ago in Germany. . . .

—If she's doing Bel Air or Beverly Hills now, you ought to think about it.

—What are you telling me, bruh?

—They take black folks in around here after dark.

I must have looked like I thought he'd slipped his harness.

—Listen, man, I'm not shooting you the shit. Beverly Hills cops do what the people want—and what they want is you and me just move out after we cut the grass or paint the fence or tend the children. Leaving in daylight is all right. Dusk is a must. After dark ain't smart.

I couldn't help laughing. Those airport voices had warned me there's no stopping in the White Zone.

—Maybe you ought to think about New Orleans, I told him. —We got a black mayor, a black chief of police . . .

—And places you best stay clear of, right?

—No, I said. —I pretty much go where I go. People who don't want me around generally got more serious reasons than color.

Henry sighed. His grandma had come West from Lafayette. He allowed as how maybe it was time to go back home.

We turned off Sunset into trees and soft streetlights, houses set so far back from the road all you saw was a porch lamp shining through the fog, a glow at some distant window.

—What about this killing tonight? he asked as he drove slow, squinting at house numbers painted on the curb. —How come Athena's rates the Secret Service?

—They got some crazy notion, I started to say.

Henry started laughing.

—Wait. I got it figured. Secret Service comes down on counterfeiting, right?

—I believe that's part of what they do.

—That little old freak got all diced up was passing *queer* in Athena's, right?

We laughed for half a block. I just kind of nodded past an answer, thinking that I was already on detached service, and Henry Harleaux would pass that joke all around the L.A.P.D. as quick as he could plug into the grapevine. It didn't seem fair to Nat Wren, but then when you go undercover calling yourself Big Bird and pinching leather, you got to take what comes. Anyhow, if that had been the worst that Nat Wren had had to suffer, I expect he'd have laughed, too.

Seventeen Bellagio Terrace was just your run-of-the-mill French chateau with tennis court, Olympic-sized swimming pool, and a six-car garage. The land alone could have gone for more than the New Orleans business district, and the grass looked like it was manicured twice a week and fertilized with chopped chicken liver. I wondered if the oaks and magnolia trees were real, or trucked in from a Studio City warehouse where they kept all the flora from *Gone with the Wind.*

Henry nodded. —So this is where the lady from Germany hangs out. Brother, keep one hand on your pistol and the other on your gun.

—I believe I can manage that.

Henry drove me past a clutch of parked Jaguars and Mercedeses and stopped before a pair of big carved double doors that stood open to welcome guests.

—You want me to stay around for a minute? Just to make sure you got the right place?

I started to tell him to move on out, but when you got right down to it, this was his town, not mine.

—Okay, that'd be a kindness. I'll come back and flag you, I said.

I could hear music from inside. Some kind of Barry Manilow crap like I used to listen to ten years ago. Nobody come when I rang the doorbell. I could hear talk and laughter coming from inside, and reckoned this was what you call informal. It had to be, since my watch read 2:47 A.M.

I went into the foyer and looked around. Marble tile floor, off-white plaster walls, ceiling higher than an antebellum uptown house in New Orleans, a crystal chandelier bigger than a jungle gym. It was a little like some nice French Quarter hotel, only portraits of Candy lined the wall beside a curving staircase that led up to the second floor.

There were rooms off the foyer in every direction, but the folksy sounds were coming from the back. Even without Henry's warning, I felt a little tight moving that deep into somebody else's house, but what the hell? If they didn't freak out and shoot, Narbonne could get me off anything softer than rape. He had to, if he wanted my invaluable cooperation.

I saw a young Latin woman in a tight black maid's uniform come out of what was likely the kitchen, carrying a tray of glasses. She headed away from me toward the party sounds, and I followed right behind her.

The French doors to a tented patio were open, and maybe a dozen people in casual clothes were sitting around an aquarium bigger than the one they were planning to build alongside the Mississippi back home. Imagine your ordinary goldfish, right? Now multiply their size by ten or fifteen. That's what was trucking around in the water at about head level as I joined the party.

—I beg your pardon, I began, and heads turned like they were tied together. I believe eyes got a little wide, too. I can't say about white knuckles. One woman managed to kill a squeal before it quite established itself, but a fat man with olive skin and watery eyes half stood up like he was thinking about running but decided he couldn't outrun me—or whatever I was packing.

You can only wait so long for somebody to speak, and I was too tired to gas around.

—Please, folks, your rings and wallets are safe. I'm trying to find Candace Prescott.

A tanned blonde who looked like she might have looked like something once stared at me.

—Candace? My God, what do you want with Candace?

I grinned. At least I was past breaking and entering. Now it was suspicion of carnal knowledge. It crossed my mind to say that if Candy wasn't available, any lady there and steaming would do just as well, but I'm too old for that silly shit. Anyhow, Candy saved me the trouble of answering. She came in wearing something she hadn't had on earlier, and even her style had changed, just a little. Without a howdy, she took me by the hand and led me over to the blonde who'd wanted to know what it was I had in mind for her.

—Mother, this is Captain Ralph Trapp. I think you remember the name.

The woman's alarmed expression faded, and she stared at

me like I'd flown in a window. Then, before I could get ready for it, she threw her arms around my neck and gave me a big kiss. She stood back and smiled like I was just what she'd been waiting for.

—I've been saving that for more than ten years, she said, turning to the others. —A long time ago, in a very dangerous place, Captain Trapp kept Candace alive. No one else could have. Captain Trapp, these are my friends and Candace's. Please feel at home among us.

Mrs. Elaine Prescott started clapping her hands, and before I could figure out how to leave, everybody else joined in. Never mind how a moment before they all thought I was there to rob them. Now I had a name and a pedigree. I was somebody.

It didn't make me mad. Why should it? If a white man walked into a black party in New Orleans, folks would want to know who he was, what he was doing there. What goes around comes around. Then it goes around again. It's gonna be a while before we walk into each other's houses expecting a smile.

After people come up and introduced themselves, Candy took me inside to a nice bar area and put a glass of John Jameson in my hand. She asked how my suit had gotten so filthy, and I filled her in on what had happened out behind Athena's. She shook her head when I told her about Nat Wren. Her eyes went wide when I mentioned the limo and that smiling bald-headed man inside.

—Jacobs? The man who . . .

—That's right, sweetie. New turf, old game.

—No, no. . . . There's no way that sonofabitch would dare turn up in the U.S. with some kind of terrorist plan. . . .

—Hey, watch what you say. The man has diplomatic status, woman.

Candy sat down in one of her momma's expensive, delicate French chairs.

—So this *is* international. The commie bastards have some kind of . . .

—Hey, honey, you're getting ahead. Maybe Jacobs was at Athena's because he likes guys. Nobody ever said the KGB was straight. Remember Hitler's boys?

She gave me this real strange look. —You still don't believe, do you? You just can't open your imagination enough to realize what . . .

—Honey, I can imagine anything. And I'm willing to admit Nat Wren just got scratched off somebody's list. But I need facts, not wild theories, to get to the bottom of this. I want to know more about Wren and those other four dead men.

—I can't . . .

—Narbonne is getting me cleared to work with youall on the case. But I don't mean to wait on the bureaucrats.

—We can't talk here. Give me five minutes.

While I went outside and sent Henry on his way, Candy went upstairs and got into some jogging clothes. She brought me a nice Dior jogging outfit, too. I didn't ask where or how or who. I mean, this is the West Coast, right?

Candy talked to me as she drove her white BMW westward down Sunset toward the Pacific Coast Highway.

—The first was Will Mohr. He was a B-movie actor. You wouldn't remember the name, but you've seen him a hundred times. The hero's best buddy. The guy who gives up the girl. Not much of a role, but he invested his earnings in some Valley real estate, and the boom after the Second World War made him rich. He and Reagan used to room together in the thirties.

—Who did what to him?

—Mohr was at the Screen Actors Guild hospital, on the respirator. Terminal emphysema. It was hardly worth the trouble, but somebody yanked the plug. They just couldn't let him die naturally. The hospital fired an orderly, but nobody can prove anything.

—And you all want to make something out of that?

Candy stared at me like I was trying to give her trouble. That wasn't what I had in mind.

—Rat, it's not the events, it's the pattern.

—What about the others?

—Next was Abe Peretz. They used to call him a whiz-kid producer at Republic back in the forties and fifties. He'd worked with Ronald Reagan on a couple of films, and they were still close. He used to fly to Washington a couple of times a year for supper at the White House. Then, a month ago, his car ran out of gas on the Hollywood Freeway. He went to an emergency phone and started to call for help. Only while he was talking, somebody ran ten feet off the road and hit him. He was smashed all to hell, dead when the California Highway Patrol got there.

—Aw, Candy, I said, weariness coming over me. —Gimme a break. . . .

—I would if I could. But the CHP got into it. Two problems: They can't find the hit-and-run driver, and Abe had filled his tank that morning.

—So he drove all over that day. . . .

—He was in his office all day.

—Anybody check the tank?

She gave me a withering look.

—Believe it or not. The tank was fine. We figure somebody had siphoned the gas out. They knew he'd be on the Freeway, and they waited . . .

Jesus, if us common cops back in New Orleans looked at every death like Candy was doing, everyone in the cemetery would be a murder victim. Still, Nat Wren was dead, as predicted by her crazy theory.

—It's the pattern that's important, Rat. Harold Swanson was

eighty-one when he was killed, the Grand Old Man of conservative politics in California. . . .

—What kind of conservative? I asked her.

—The usual kind. He didn't want to pay any taxes. Everything else was negotiable.

—What did he do?

—He was a lawyer—and a close friend of former President Reagan. Part of what they used to call "the kitchen cabinet" when Reagan was governor.

—What happened to him?

—They found Swanson drowned in his Jacuzzi, smelling like a distillery.

—That happens out here, don't it?

—You bet, and that's how they were writing it up . . . only somebody in the medical examiner's office had time on his hands and ran a blood test and a few other medical things.

—What?

—Turns out there wasn't any blood alcohol. In fact, the only place they found alcohol was in his mouth.

That woke me up. We knew that move in New Orleans. Sometimes people got to be inconvenient to the mob. Nothing personal. They were just in the way. They'd get good liquor poured down their throats just before the water closed over their heads. Except home they used Lake Pontchartrain or the Mississippi River instead of a Jacuzzi.

—Did that make the papers?

—No, the Service got interested about then, and Al put a muzzle on the M.E. Not even Swanson's family saw the autopsy report.

—Who was next?

—Louis Werner. He used to be an executive at Warner Brothers back in the forties and fifties. Then he went into the fund-raising business for conservative causes, and he was great at it. Guess for who? His Cessna crashed in the Pacific almost on top of a tuna fisherman. Werner was naked. So was the girl with him. The plane was on auto-pilot and ran out of fuel.

—Well now, that's new. I never heard that one before. Accident?

—Same as Swanson. It looked like an old fool fooled himself right out of it. Except the M.E. looked again. No water in the lungs. Both of the victims were pumped full of heroin and dead before that plane hit the water.

—You got that M.E. down for the Medal of Freedom?

—He's got two points.

—Okay, you've got me convinced. The deaths all fit the same pattern. Someone very creative and resourceful killed those five old men on purpose—and Camille by accident. But who? And why?

We drove north on Pacific Coast Highway, past Malibu and Zuma Beach. The sun was just coming up as we crossed the Ventura county line and parked at a deserted beachfront eatery called Neptune's Net.

Candy said it was a spot favored by surfers. We followed a path down a sandy cliff to a nice little beach. There was still a good stiff onshore breeze from the storm that had passed through the night before. The waves were crashing up on the sand, and the sky was going from midnight blue to gray.

Houses huddled near the water at one end of the beach, but the sandy expanse was deserted, and the far reaches of the chill Pacific were still dark and invisible. Behind us, the Santa Monica Mountains were turning gold on their peaks, and except for being dog-tired, I thought this was a better place for my morning run than St. Charles Avenue or even Audubon Park.

The sand was hard and damp, and it felt good to pound along the edge of the white, hissing water with a good-looking woman beside me.

Candy's running gear was thin and tight, and I could see her body moving under the slick cloth. I didn't know how she was feeling, but I was getting that old edge on about her. I had thoughts of dropping down next to a pile of weathered rock at the edge of the surf and doing that old *From Here to Eternity* number just like Burt and Deborah did when I was a kid growing up. Then the memory of Camille calling out my name over that microphone prodded me, and I kept moving.

Finally, Candy fell exhausted on the sand, turned on her back, and caught the first rays of the sun on her body. It was already working-time in New Orleans, and I was feeling a night without sleep and the time differential, too. I sat down beside her as an old woman in a short skirt came from the direction of the houses, walking a dog with shaggy hair who liked to run into the surf and then shake himself before heading for the water again.

As Candy struggled to get her breath back I brought out a Marsh-Wheeling cigar I'd stuck in my pocket when I changed at her momma's house. Candy looked like she wanted to make some kind of comment when I lit it up. Bad for the health. But then, when you make a living getting shot at, little piss-ant business like a cigar now and again don't seem like much. The old broad with the shaggy dog came back past us and gave me a look. I got the feeling she wanted to say something, too, but she passed on by.

—If we only had witnesses—even one witness, Candy said. —But every one of those old men died solo, or whoever they were with died, too.

I thought about that. I couldn't say about the rest, but Nat Wren's case was a little different.

—Wren might show us something, I said.

—What? Was there a witness in that parking lot?

—No, but according to your theory, that wasn't the first time they tried for him.

Candy sat up and stared at me.

—That's right. That accident that killed Camille Bynum was meant for Nat. . . .

—And there were a couple hundred witnesses—and a film crew, too.

—A what?

—Somebody was filming the whole business. When I got there, I saw this camera, a crew . . .

Candy reached over and gave me a kiss. It wasn't a prelude to *From Here to Eternity*. More like *Bikini Beach Party*.

—My God, then somewhere there's a film of what happened.

—Yeah, I said, feeling suddenly dark. —A film of Camille dying with that shorted mike in her hand. I've already seen that. I don't need to see it again.

—But if that cameraman panned the crowd, Rat, there's no telling . . .

She rose to her feet, ready to run again. This time back toward her BMW.

—Come on, she yelled over her shoulder at me. —Come on. We'll call Al and get his help finding who was filming.

As we neared Neptune's Net I could see another car had pulled into the empty parking space beside hers. A black Chrysler New Yorker. The door of her BMW was open and a man was leaning inside, like he was hot-wiring it—or checking the registration. I yelled out, and he straightened. Then he leaned across the hood, and pointed something lethal-looking at us.

I lunged at Candy and caught her ankles. We crashed together on the sand as the sound of the first shots reached us. Assault rifle on full automatic.

—Roll, I shouted, and obeyed my own order. We wedged ourselves tight up against the sandy bank. Sand sprayed over us as, above our heads, slugs chopped away at the earth protecting us. Shit. I'd left my Magnum locked in the trunk of

Candy's BMW when we took off jogging down the beach. There was nothing to do but push Candy's head into the sand and play ostrich myself.

Then there was silence. The shooter had emptied his magazine. Would he reload and come after us? Did he realize the lack of return fire meant we were unarmed, or did he think I was trying to sucker him into breaking cover?

From a house behind us, I heard a dog yapping excitedly and then a high-pitched woman's voice yelling out. —I'm calling the sheriff's office. There's a law against shooting guns on the beach. . . .

I guess the shooter didn't like to work in front of a crowd. We heard the man's car start and lay rubber as it sped away south on the coast highway. I stuck my head up over the edge of the bank and tried to make the license, but whoever had been tailing us had been more careful than Jacobs' driver. The back plate of the fast-disappearing Chrysler was covered with mud.

Candy lifted her head. Damp grains of sand clung to her face like a mask. I guess I looked like a reverse Al Jolson myself. She brushed sand from her hair and spit grit from her mouth.

—The lady's right, she said wryly. —California has strict laws against discharging firearms, even shotguns.

I held up a pellet I'd dug out of the bank in front of us. —Fuck shotguns. This is an AK-47-m slug.

—A KGB favorite. Jacobs must have thought you saw too much. Could you have been followed from Athena's?

—Only by a professional. But then, that's what we're supposed to be dealing with here, ain't it?

I had my Colt Cobra tucked comfortably back in my shoulder holster when Candy drove us into the Beverly Hills commercial district, where the parking meters are goldplated and shirts go for $225. They called the place we were headed Nate 'n Al's, and if you like deli, welcome home.

I picked up a taste for sausages and such during my tour of duty in Germany, and when I walked through the door, there was that old-time smell put together out of dill pickles and rye bread, pastrami, and fifty kinds of cheese. New Orleans has fine food, but deli's not what they do. Even with all the bullshit going down, I could see the day was gonna go all right—even if I hadn't seen a bed in twenty hours or so.

The place was already crowded at 8:15 in the morning. Candy told me the men in jogging suits or hand-tailored denims who filled the booths were talking deals that might or might not happen, selling scripts and talent and locations and concepts. By the cash register were stacks of *The Hollywood Reporter* and *Daily Variety*—trade journals written in a foreign tongue a lot harder to get hold of than what they used to call "black English."

—There he is, Candy said, pointing toward a back booth.

Narbonne was sitting with a cup of coffee and a couple of brown Manila envelopes in front of him, fidgeting, playing like reading the *L.A. Times*. When he saw us, he dropped the paper and looked all business.

—You've been cleared, Rat. And I spoke to Major Mauvais at N.O.P.D. You belong to us for two weeks.

—I got to call and thank him.

—No, he said I could have you for two years if I wanted to pick up your salary.

—He was putting you on. The man's like a father to me.

Narbonne did his shrug. —Major Mauvais said there hasn't been a cop shooting anybody since you left town.

—I go out of the parish limits, and they all sit on their asses and shirk their duty. Don't sweat it. I can catch up when I get back.

Narbonne forced a laugh, but you could see he was wondering just how funny it was. You don't do it every day, you miss the humor.

The waitress poured us cups of some thin, light-brown wood stain they call coffee in the rest of the country, and I told Narbonne about the rounds of shots we'd taken.

—Okay, Narbonne said, pocketing the slug, —I'll have it run through the lab. Here's what we got on the Soviet consulate's office.

He fanned out a set of photos across the table. I was surprised at how good they were. Some were standard ID photos, what you'd expect on a passport. Others had been taken at social gatherings, meetings, even on the street. I went through them carefully. He wasn't there. I never reckoned he was gonna be there.

—Sorry, I said. —You just hired me for nothing. If that's the consulate, our boy has him another venue.

Narbonne wasn't concerned. He pushed the photos aside and opened another envelope.

—These are all the Russian nationals or recent émigrés in California who come close to the description you and Candy gave of Jacobs.

We both looked them over, dozens of them. I didn't know we'd let so many of those buggers in.

—You follow émigrés around snapping pictures of 'em, seeing what they're up to?

Narbonne tried to smile. —That's absurd, and illegal.

—Right, I said. —He ain't here, is he, Candy?

She shook her head. —Not even close.

Narbonne nodded again. Still cool, still unconcerned. His last envelope was thin. It had one picture in it. He held it back, then flipped it between us face up like he was trumping a trick.

It was a blowup of a blurred black-and-white photo of three young soldiers in Soviet uniforms standing amid ruins, over an open pit full of ashes and rubble. In the distance behind, next to a fallen wall, was one lonely scraggly tree. Don't ask how I recognized the place, but I did.

—Rat, Candy said, pointing to one of the Russians, her voice quavering just the least bit, —could that be him?

I nodded. Maybe. Not certain, but possible. The young soldier had hair, and his face was the round, unseasoned face of a boy. No matter what he had done, what he had seen, it was still the face of a boy. Standing in the Reichschancellery garden over a pit of ashes that belonged to Adolf Hitler and some others.

—How in the hell did you guys get hold of this?

Narbonne grinned as he picked up the picture and studied it carefully. —Jacobs, Blue Section, KGB. Reputed never to have been photographed in his life. But we got this. Taken May second, 1945, outside the Bunker. He was a commissar then. Third Rifle Regiment of the Leningrad Guards . . .

His voice died away as he looked at the photo almost lovingly. —So it *is* him.

—You weren't sure? Candy asked in surprise.

—Not which one. We didn't have the photo twelve years ago, and nobody remembered you'd seen Jacobs up close when it surfaced. Things get lost in the cracks. But we always pick them up again down the road.

—Hell, I said. —It's a nice move, but what does it mean? That damn picture is forty and more years old. He's changed some.

—That's all right. It's a baseline.

—Baseline?

—We can computer-generate Colonel Jacobs just about the way he looks now.

Narbonne put all the pictures away, looking plumb gleeful.

—I believe I've got something coming now, Alphonse, I reminded him.

—You want our files on the other victims?

—Naw, Candy filled me in on the important stuff. I mean, the badge and some credentials. See, I want to go dropping my weight around like a 900-pound gorilla. I got to practice how you pop out that I.D.-card case and snarl when you say, "Secret Service . . ."

Narbonne surprised me. He slipped a nice dark-brown I.D. case across the table. There I was inside. He must have had New Orleans fax him a copy of my police I.D. picture. It was five years old. I was thinner and meaner then.

I tucked it away and reached for my menu. Narbonne stopped me.

—Forget that, Rat. You want the corned beef hash.

—Don't they serve bologna and pastrami sandwiches, New York potato salad and dills on the side, this early?

—They serve that stuff all the time. But you want the corned beef hash with a couple of eggs on top.

I could see my vision of a five-inch-high sandwich dissolving. Narbonne knew the place, and he knew me. If he said the hash, I had to try the hash. Maybe I could keep this meeting going long enough to pick up on a sandwich after the hash.

After the waitress took Candy's order, she turned to me.

—Corned beef hash with a pair straight up on top.

—Tomato or hashed-browns?

—Gimme the potatoes.

—Bagel, Kaiser roll, or toast?

—Toast.

—Rye, pumpernickel, or white?

—Uh . . . white.

—Butter, margarine, or plain?

—Jesus, lady . . . buttered.

She gave us a nice businesslike smile and marched away. Even Candy was laughing quietly.

—And you think you know how to handle an interrogation, Narbonne grinned.

The service was fast, and we ate more or less in silence. After we were done, I decided to let the sandwich go on by. I was considering another order of the hash. No way to describe it. It's up there with Galatoire's oysters en brochette or T. Alonso's stuffed crab. I kind of shook my head. Who expects a world-class meal in L.A.?

When the next round of coffee came, Candy brought up the camera crew I'd seen at the Hollywood Boulevard sidewalk star business. Narbonne frowned and stared into his notebook.

—What camera crew?

Candy looked at me.

—There was a film crew shooting everything that happened, I told him.

—The cops missed them, Narbonne said. —Could it have been a TV news crew?

—Not unless TV is going back to film, I said.

—Goddamn L.A.P.D. They couldn't track a blind elephant in a snowstorm with his throat cut.

—They probably didn't think it mattered, Candy told him. —Nobody notices a camera setup on Hollywood Boulevard. They're like fireplugs or telephone poles.

Al Narbonne was keeping his temper. —Finish your coffee, people. We've got to do our work—and the L.A.P.D.'s, too.

It turned out the L.A.P.D. hadn't drawn a complete blank. Someone had recorded the license numbers of all the limos and cars within the blocked-off area. One was leased by di Silva Productions.

Inside a couple of hours, Candy and I were in my new undercover car. No, it wasn't a 1982 black Olds Cutlass with a dent in the driver's door and some bullet holes puttied and painted. It was an '89 Mercedes-Benz 500SL convertible. Who told you I work cheap? He's a lying sonofabitch.

We were out in the West Side again, back in Candy's momma's neighborhood, looking for the address di Silva Productions had given the car rental company.

—They got an office in Bel Air? I asked her.

—A lot of independent producers work out of their homes. Alexander Graham Bell didn't invent the phone—some agent or producer did.

Candy pointed me to a secluded street called Mountain Way. It was lined with pines and eucalyptus and even a few magnolias that looked like they'd come West and done all right. The house was back off the road, a kind of chalet with exposed beams and the mandatory six-car garage.

Candy said something into a phone box at the gate and it slid quietly open. When we neared the house, I saw a stretch limo with some tall muscular guy washing it down. Was it one of the limos I'd seen on Hollywood Boulevard? Hell, they got more stretch limos than Chevies in Bel Air, and every one the same color looks like every other one.

We pulled up a little distance from the front door. The guy washing the limo stopped and gave us a long careful look. He had dark hair and a handlebar mustache. When I stared back at him, his eyes hooked into mine and stayed there. We played dogs in the alley for a minute, then he went back to work. Ole Handlebar Mustache didn't break the look because I made him uncomfortable, and that made *me* uncomfortable. What was a guy like that doing washing cars? He belonged in Brooklyn or Miami washing money.

A maid in a close-fitting black dress and a white cap answered our ring. I forgot the chauffeur or whatever he was. This little bitty lady was stone fine. Black hair, large dark eyes, a face that made you think of round mattresses and mirrored ceilings—a five-foot-ten-inch woman on a five-two frame. She looked back at me and smiled. Yeah, I thought, that's the way all the guys look at you.

I popped my I.D. case on her for the first time. That smile didn't leave, but it froze in place.

—Mr. di Silva, I asked.

She looked at me for a long moment, smile still lurking, but those eyes moving across my face like sensors.

—There is no Signore di Silva, she said with a rich, light Italian accent. —Signore is . . . dead. Six months now.

—Sorry. Who runs the place?

—Signora di Silva, but . . .

—That's who we want to see.

—She sees very few people. . . .

—You tell the lady she can talk to us here and now—or later. Down at the federal building.

The smile was gone then, like one minute after sunset. My

little doll could make those dark eyes as cold as a snowdrift in the Alps. She disappeared upstairs. When I turned to Candy, she was looking me over like she'd never seen me before.

—God, it didn't take you long.

—Huh?

—You sound like a fed. First time out of the box.

—Well, see, darlin', I consort with murderers and pimps, liars and freaks, dopeheads and child molesters. Put 'em all together, and you know just what an officer of the United States is supposed to sound like.

She was still laughing when my little Latin cupcake come back and told me what I knew she'd tell me all along.

Signora di Silva was nodding backward at eighty years, and if she got any uglier, they were gonna escort her out of Bel Air in a limo with one-way glass. Wrinkles inside wrinkles. Her face looked like a relief map of the Santa Monica Mountains.

She wore one of those 1920s turbans wrapped around her head, but it wasn't that fashion-time had stopped for her when she was a young girl. It was that she didn't have any more hair. Her skin wasn't tan or brown, it was dark ashy gray, and along her arms it hung in folds and layers on small fragile birdlike bones. You could snap her arm with your fingers, and break her neck with one light chop beneath her ear. She was an awful warning about what great age brings us.

And yet that wasn't the whole package. Behind heavy grainy lids, she still had two dark, shining eyes that looked like she'd bought or stolen them from the twenty-year-old sister of her maid. The rest was rubble and decay and nineteen portents of doom. But the Signora had her a pair of eyes.

Those eyes moved from me to Candy and back again, as if she was trying to figure out whether she knew us, should know us, wanted to know us.

—Anna Maria say you must see me. You are federals?

—Yes, ma'am, I answered smoothly.

I couldn't tell if the old lady still had wind in her sails, but you play it from the middle. Be bland for openers. Always time to move some other way.

—What we need to know is, did you have some folks working over on Hollywood Boulevard, late afternoon, three days ago?

I guessed she was smiling. No way to be sure. Maybe she couldn't handle her mouth muscles anymore. She didn't say anything for what seemed a long time. That was all right. I never get antsy. I make other people antsy.

—Ahhh, she said finally. —That. Where the accident overcame the poor lady . . .

—Yeah, I said. —That's when.

—It was for my husband.

—Huh?

—Di Silva is dead.

—Your maid mentioned that. Sorry.

—This . . . ummm, that was his last wish. A film about Hollywood.

It went on like that in fits and starts. The old lady was still more or less together, but she had trouble with her English and jump-starting her memory sometimes. It was all there. You just had to take it at her pace. Why not? If I don't get my ass blown off, one day I'm gonna be a shriveled-up old black man with a silver halo trying to tell some nephew or cousin twice removed how I once faced down a KGB colonel.

The old lady told us her husband had been a very bigtime Italian director and producer. He'd fallen in love with the movies when he was a little boy, had gotten into the business in Rome early on. You name it, he'd done it. Even a documentary—believe it or not—on how the Duce made the trains run on time.

But it had always seemed at second remove to him. Making movies in Rome or Florence or Turin wasn't really making movies. Movies are made in Hollywood, California. Now it was Hollywood's seventy-fifth anniversary, and Carlo di Silva had come over to see his true hometown and to make his last documentary—a tribute to tinsel town.

He was in Los Angeles, in this lovely leased house that had once belonged to Douglas Fairbanks, Sr., less than three weeks when, in the presence of such greatness, his heart failed him. That's what she said, not me.

Candy was moved. —You're continuing his project?

Signora di Silva nodded, those eyes melting, obscuring the age, the wattles, the flabby skin for a moment.

—There is this great thing we came to do. It must be finished.

It crossed my mind she'd better hurry. But then I didn't know how much she had to do or how long it would take.

The old lady explained that her husband's documentary, this tribute to Hollywood, would be made up of interviews with people who had spent their lives in the business, scenes from old films, shots of studios and locations, and what she called rituals of the place—like setting a star in Hollywood's Walk of Fame.

Candy explained what we were after. A copy of the film they'd shot on Hollywood Boulevard, so that we could look over the accident again.

—Of course, of course. You're federal inspectors. You want to punish the electrician, the old lady said.

—That's exactly right. I smiled back at her vagueness. —I want me a piece of that electrician.

She picked up a crystal bell from the table beside her. When my little Italian charmer turned up, Signora rattled off something faster than my ears work. The maid left the room without looking at either of us.

Candy started filling in the time. —Actually, the lady who was killed was close to Captain Trapp. . . .

I wondered what the hell she was getting into that for.

Signora looked at me. —This woman who die? She was important to you?

—Yeah, I said. —You could put it that way. . . .

—Then . . . this is not what you call . . . official?

Candy cut in before I could say anything.

—Official . . . unofficially, Signora.

The old lady nodded understanding—which is more than I could do.

—Of course, of course. Sometimes in the night, I put on films of my husband, bring him back to me, look at his face. . . . Maybe I pretend he is still alive.

There was more of that kind of talk, then the maid returned with a reel of film in her hand. She gave us a quick look and whispered something to the Signora. She nodded and passed the film to me.

—Don't look at the bad part, Signor. Find your stills when she was alive, when death was . . . the farthest thing from her mind.

I nodded. It was nice advice. I was already wishing I could follow it as we made a moment more of conversation, then our good-byes, and headed back into the California sun where everything was alive, and the idea of death seemed something imported from back East.

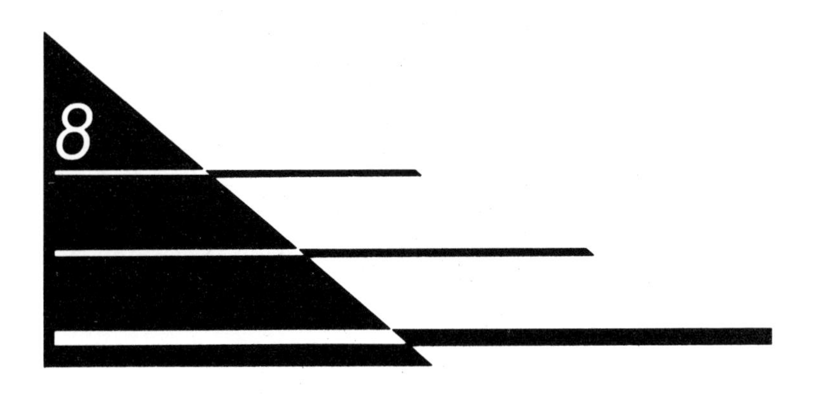

Back in my Mercedes then, with the top down, looking like one of those dimbulbs who made his bucks a dozen years ago in blaxploitation movies. I was starting out of Bel Air, figuring to check in with Narbonne at the special Secret Service office they'd set up on Wilshire Boulevard, when Candy put her hand on my arm.

—We're close to Mother's. Why don't we stop there?

—Narbonne is gonna want to see the film.

—Mother has a projector. I'd really like to make sure my father's not a face in the crowd.

I reached over and patted her thigh.

—No problem, baby. And it gives us a leg up on all our government colleagues, too, don't it?

I could see Candy wanted a starring role in the Beltway Follies. Whatever had driven her to join the Company a dozen years ago was still whipping her to the front of the pack. She was determined to go as fast and as far as she could. And a daddy the feds suspected of running around in a long cloak and broad-brimmed hat with a bomb in one hand and a match in the other was a downright embarrassment.

I parked in the driveway of the Prescott house again. In daylight, the house looked even bigger, more imposing than it had at night. I wondered how many rooms the place had, and what use one woman alone had for so much space.

—What split your folks up? I asked Candy. Her expression made me wish I could swallow the question.

—Everything. Nothing.

I nodded as we got out and walked half a block to the front door. I wasn't gonna poke around in Candy's family cellar any more. One question too many was enough. So let it go.

Candy was opening the door with her key as the Latino maid turned up. I thought the sweet thing would show us what closet the projector was in, but it seemed a little more complicated than that. Candy handed her the reel of film and motioned me to follow her down a long softly lit hallway hung with paintings I almost recognized. We stepped into a room with maybe twenty theater seats in it. I could hear the maid fooling around in a projection room behind us.

—Jesus, don't anybody just look at TV out here?

—No one I know, she answered with a tight little smile as she closed the drapes, shutting out a view of the pool and lawn and trees beyond. I moved over to a small bar where fresh ice was waiting in a gold bucket.

Before the next hour had passed, I needed the whiskey. I could have skipped the ice.

I saw it all happening again on a 4 × 5 screen, skillfully filmed, in living color. I saw her arriving by limo, smiling and beautiful, being greeted by Nat Wren, led to the seat of honor on the platform. Speakers I didn't know were praising Danny. Then the part I had lived through started. I saw Camille rising, taking the mike to call out to me. I saw her dying second after second.

Then, right then, something incredible happened. I was sitting in a dark theater with a glass of Irish in my hand, watching myself. I was pushing aside the crowd, jumping up onto the stage, drawing my weapon, firing down into the junction box. I was turning to lower Camille to the floor, my face twisting in agony as I held her burned hand, looked into her staring sightless eyes. Jesus, I was seeing myself at the worst moment of my life. Here I was watching from outside, there I was dying inside.

See, that's Hollywood. Makes you a peeping freak on your own life. I finished off the Irish and closed my eyes. I wanted to be back at the Acme Oyster Bar in the Quarter with Wes Colvin, bragging and telling lies, knowing in some back alley of my mind that Camille was out there in L.A. alive and well, eating at Spago's or some other dumb-assed place, happy as she could be.

When the film played through and the lights came up, I heard Candy clear her throat.

—I didn't see Daddy . . . or Jacobs, she said in a small apologetic voice. —I didn't see anything we can use.

—No, I said, my eyes snapping open, my legs lifting me as I headed for the bar. —Nothing we can use. . . .

Candy joined me and poured my glass full.

—Rat, I'm so sorry. It was as bad as it can be. God, even at secondhand . . .

I took a good slug and moved back to my seat.

—Tell your girl to run it again. This time, I'll try to see.

—Are you sure you want to look at . . . ?

—Play it again, Samantha, I called back to the projection booth behind.

The lights went down, and that piece of my life started in again. But no matter how many times we played that goddamned film over, I'd never make better time up to the platform, knock the microphone out of Camille's hand, save the lady, and take my bow.

The second time through, though, the pain was already receding. I was looking out at the margins of the shots, trying to see anybody or anything unusual. While Camille jerked and twitched at center stage, I was working, not dying with her like at the performance and the first time through the film.

But like Candy said, no Jacobs. Nobody who even looked like one of his people. That platform was already up when the film began. I couldn't see anybody doing anything suspicious that might have made the equipment fall. Just Nat Wren watching in horror, his hands over his face, as Camille danced to the pulse of the current and died. As the cameraman turned away from the horror, the last frames showed a glimpse of Signora di Silva sitting in the back seat of her limo with that big tall mustached joker who had been washing her car at the wheel.

As the film went black I became aware somebody had opened the door to the lighted hall behind us.

—Too bad that dirty cringing little faggot Wren didn't fry, Elaine Prescott said.

She switched on the lights, and I saw her face twisted in hatred and some old rage that time hadn't managed to obscure.

—Mother? Candy said in a shocked voice.

—Somebody else thinks like you, Ms. Prescott, I said. —Wren was offed last night. In a parking lot behind a queer bar in West Hollywood.

—That's good news. Candace, open the drapes. I want to fix a drink . . . to celebrate.

Elaine Prescott began splashing vodka into a martini pitcher at the bar as Candy opened the drapes and let the California sunshine pour in. The years showed more than they had at the party last night, but Candy's mother was still quite a dish.

—I didn't know you even knew Nat Wren, Candy said. —What makes you so . . . ?

—He ruined everything. He ruined it for Milt and me. And for you, too. Oh, goddamn his soul. . . .

Her hands were trembling as she tossed down a straight-up martini and set her glass down for another one.

—But for Wren, Milt and I might have made it. People with less going for them did.

Candy looked at her mother with an expression of amazement.

—You always said the marriage was impossible. That you couldn't live with Daddy after . . .

—Oh, honey, when Milt and I married, everything was possible. We'd just won the war. There wasn't ever going to be another. Your father was writing for Warner's. He'd been nominated for an Oscar for *Meeting at the Elbe.* A wonderful film about an American sergeant and a Russian lieutenant . . .

Elaine Prescott's face lost that moment of illumination. It wasn't 1946 anymore. It was later.

—Then the goddamned politicians started in. God, three years before, Glenn Miller was calling them our fighting Russian allies and playing "The Volga Boatman." If Miller had lived through the war, they'd have ruined him, too.

—You're saying Milt Hebron was a target in the McCarthy hearings? I asked.

—Nobody had ever heard of McCarthy then, Elaine answered me. —When the House Un-American Activities Committee came to Hollywood, they were just dumpy little men from back East in suits that didn't fit. And of course all of them hated us. During all the questioning and the hearings, you could smell the envy. California was the Golden Land. We lived our lives in the sun, and we had money and fame and estates bigger than some of their towns—and despite all that, we thought Left.

Candy didn't buy. —That was just a silly Hollywood game my father played, she hastily explained to me. —He and his friends were Limousine Liberals, Parlor Pinks . . .

Elaine looked like she was going to throw her third martini

in her daughter's face. —You don't know what you're talking about.

She turned to me as if asking me to referee. —Captain Trapp, Milt believed in peoples' rights. He wrote scripts that stood up for Negroes and Orientals, for Mexicans and those poor ignorant farm workers who'd flooded in here from Oklahoma and Texas. . . .

Candy looked sullen. Me? I was just wondering what "standing up" meant and pouring myself another drink.

—The truth is, my daddy . . . was called a traitor, Candy said in a voice filled with emotion. —A Communist.

I'll be damned. So that's what had been driving Candy so hard for so many years. Maybe if she went CIA, and risked her life for her country, people might forget what they'd said about her father in the fifties.

—Milt never joined the Party, Elaine answered defensively. —He just wanted to see things get better . . . for everyone.

—If he was all that wonderful, why did you walk out? Why did you leave him and take me with you?

Elaine Prescott's cool Bel Air manner faltered then. She didn't look like a natural-bred winner anymore. Just like a nice lady of sixty who had settled her accounts, whatever they were, and had in mind to live out the rest of whatever life she had left having nice parties with a few old friends. When she spoke, I could hardly hear her.

—Because I wasn't strong enough to stay. Because of what they did to us. Because of that dirty little animal Nat Wren and all the rest of them . . .

I began to feel like I didn't belong there. It became a woman telling her daughter a long sad story from years before, what had happened under this same startling California sun to a lot of people who wrote movies and starred in movies and made movies and sold movies and didn't know shit about a world you couldn't skew a little with special effects or the change of a line of dialogue.

But they both accepted my being there, so I sipped my whiskey and listened to some Hollywood history.

Nat Wren had been a half-assed agent who had friends where it counted and got named public relations officer for the House Un-American Activities Committee when it came West in '51 to see why Hollywood kept making all those movies that said Communism was a fine idea.

Wren had been the point man. He knew everybody, and he knew what they had done and who they'd done it with. He'd been a valuable man to HUAC—like a pointer to a bird hunter. He'd name a name to the committee and tell them what the dingbat had done, who his associates were, how they'd all served the Commie cause.

When Nat pointed his finger, the committee would issue a subpoena, and, as quick as it was served, Nat was on the doorstep telling the poor dingbat who was summoned that the HUAC hearings were gonna be the gateway to hell.

Those who resisted and tried to play Fifth Amendment mind games with the committee weren't ever gonna work in Hollywood again. It was gonna be a crusade, and you were either in or out. When Congress was done with all the hunting and pecking, Hollywood was gonna be clean, All-American, creating All-American films for an All-American audience who wanted to be told that the war they'd just bled their way through was only half the game—that with the Nazis wiped out, there was still one more disease germ left to exterminate: Communism.

But Nat had spent too many years on the edge of things, watching the Hollywood rich and wanting to be one of them, not to have something going for himself while he was doing his patriotic duty. He offered the dingbats a way out: All you had to do was confess your sins, do penance by naming all your buddies who had waltzed with the Party—and sign up with the Nat Wren Agency after you got your clean bill of health.

If you were signed with Nat Wren, everybody in town would know where you stood. If you didn't sign with Nat, maybe you'd better sign on as a truck driver or a carpenter—because you sure as hell weren't gonna be acting or writing or directing when HUAC was done doing what it had in mind to do.

And one day, Nat Wren had come to Milt Hebron.

—Milt had just written *Under the Double Eagle,* Elaine told us. —A fine script about labor violence in the Western mining camps after the Civil War. The people who'd seen it in editing were telling him he'd finally win his Oscar. Then Wren told Milt the Bearden committee had him made for his service in Spain.

—His service with the International Brigade? I asked.

—Yes. Wren said that was enough to keep Milt from working anywhere in town again, unless he came across. . . .

—Came across?

—They wanted names. They wanted Party members from the thirties, anyone who'd served in Spain with the Loyalists—especially officers.

—What did your husband do?

—He told Wren to screw himself. The next day, Warner Brothers told Milt that either he cooperated with the committee or he was out of work—permanently.

Candy was looking unhappy. —He should have testified.

—Milt wouldn't betray his friends. When he picked up his last check, a security guard tore up his pass and escorted Milt off the lot. I don't think he's ever been inside a studio since.

—He started his bookstore then? I asked.

—No. That came later. At first we had some savings to live on. Milt spent his time speaking at meetings denouncing the committee, writing manifestos proclaiming that no one was going to watch Hollywood movies made by Fascist studios. He wrote pieces for Leftist papers and magazines. Sometimes he even got paid a little. But after a while, no one wanted to hear about HUAC anymore. What had happened to Milt and the others who were blackballed was too bad, but what's the pain of a few compared to the misery of the many?

—Those Left bastards, Candy said with feeling.

Elaine Prescott smiled wearily, as if to say you can get awful tired of knowing something for thirty years.

—Everyone is a bastard, honey. Even Milt. In the end, life illegitimizes all of us. Your father refused to do something awful to his old Leftist friends. He chose to do something awful to me and to himself, instead.

—What do you mean?

Elaine Prescott paused as if she was wondering whether to go on or fluff it off. Maybe I knew what she was going to do before she did. But then I wasn't quite in the same situation she was. Lack of sleep and good whiskey had made a small-time mystic out of me.

—He couldn't get work in Hollywood, except for bootleg fix-it work on other writers' scripts. So he dragged us all over the country. First to New Jersey. He hoped to land an editing job with a book publisher but ended up driving a taxi. After that he wrote ad copy for the *Cleveland Plain Dealer* awhile. Then Hodding Carter gave him a little job on the *Delta Democrat-Times* in Mississippi. That might have amounted to something, but Milt got a rent strike started. Three Negroes were killed before they stopped it. And when they did, they came after us. You were only four.

I could see Candy remembered none of this. It was like hearing somebody else's history—except it wasn't somebody else's. It was her family's.

—My dad, your grandfather, sent me a train ticket with meals in the diner paid. He wouldn't send cash because he thought I'd use it to bail out that "dirty Jew Bolshevik" I'd been damned fool enough to marry.

Suddenly, Elaine looked at us both with a bright awful smile that went no deeper than her eyes.

—He needn't have worried. I took you to the train station and retched in the lady's room and washed myself all over with paper towels till I thought my skin was coming off. Then I caught the train for California and didn't think of Milt till after Daddy's car and driver brought us back here. You see? I was a bastard, too.

She got up then and walked away from us, back toward the bar. Candy and I sat there saying nothing at all, thinking of the political spasms that had sent her mother and the old man at the bookstore from Hollywood to Mississippi, with stops between.

Then Elaine Prescott came back, another martini in her hand. She looked at us with a pained brittle smile.

—I've hurt you, baby, and I've bored Captain Trapp, she said. —I'm terribly sorry. It all happened so long ago, I can't imagine why it still . . . seems to matter so much. Whatever else, those awful times gave us you.

Elaine Prescott leaned down and kissed Candy's cheek. Candy started to say something, but she caught herself.

There was nothing for me to say, either. Lord knows I hadn't been bored, but I wasn't learning anything I could use, either. Mrs. Prescott lifted her glass to us in a pallid little toast and walked unsteadily out of the room.

Candy saw me to the door in silence. I could see she was turning over in her mind what she'd just learned.

—I knew Daddy had always had Leftist sympathies, that he'd refused to testify before the HUAC, but I never realized just how deeply. . . . I see now why the Agency wanted me here, to probe him and his contacts.

—Come on, Candy. I can't believe these killings were committed by feckless old men and women who can't let go of the past.

—At least none of Daddy's friends showed up on that film, she said with relief.

—What do you want to do with it?

She said she'd take it to Narbonne's office, so I drove myself back to the Roosevelt for some rest.

My room was dark, the drapes pulled closed over the sliding glass door that looked out on the pool with its silly painted bottom. Like they say, when my head hit the pillow . . .

The dreams came and went. You know what dreams can do. They can take you back to old times like Elaine Prescott's memories did her—or send you off into some kind of personal fantasy that terrifies or satisfies.

I was with a woman. It could have been Camille or Candy—or both or neither. We were in Desire Project—or a Falangist cell, or a camp in the Gulag—or maybe even a tank town jail in Mississippi. We were in love, and we knew it wasn't gonna happen because, for whatever reason, they were gonna kill us, cut us down like suckers off a tree trunk. There was nothing we could do about it. There was nothing they wanted except for us to die. And now, even at that moment, they were coming. We could hear their footsteps coming. We held each other, then the cell or wire enclosure or whatever it was opened, and I came flailing up out of the depths of sleep, a swimmer whose last breath is flowing out of his lungs like blood from a wound.

—Captain Trapp, the bald man with red eyebrows sitting on the side of my bed with an automatic aimed at my throat was saying with just a trace of accent. —It's been a long time.

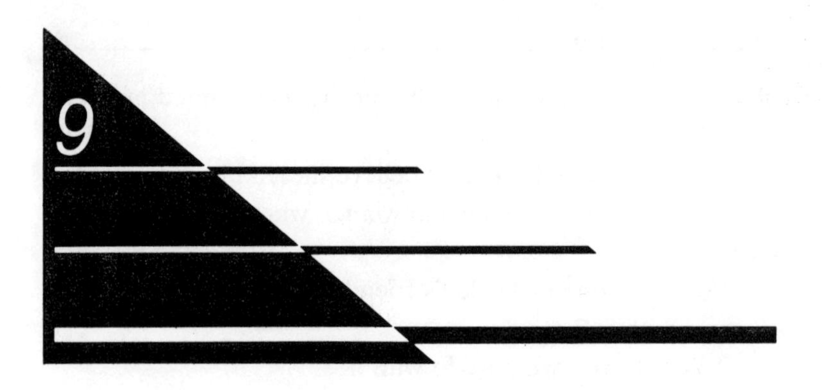

9

He put the pistol into his belt and stood up, moving away from the bed.

—A precaution only. Some men wake up . . . in a troubled mood, Jacobs was saying as he took a bright metal flask out of his pocket and poured something into a pair of glasses he'd lifted from my bathroom.

I pushed off the dream and shook out the sleep without too much alarm. Since he had let me wake up, I had to believe he wanted to talk instead of kill me.

—Old Polish brandy, he said as I threw down my glassful. I managed not to choke or even gasp. —Some people like it very much. Some don't.

—Over here, timber rattlers pack the same juice, I said.

—Ah, good. You like it. Word has it, your Secret Service wants to see me. . . .

—Yeah, well, after the other night next to that dumpster, the whole fucking U.S. bureaucracy is looking for you, old son.

—That's why I came to you. . . .

—Want to give me another poke of that stuff? I got to get lucid.

Jacobs smiled and poured. —I think we're all alcoholics in the trade.

—Lady a few hours ago told me we were all bastards.

—Taken for granted. All bastards striving for legitimacy. Whatever that is.

—Maybe it's getting out from under all those other poor bastards you've murdered since the Revolution.

—Or the American Indians, the blacks, the workers. . . .

—Like the lady was saying . . .

We both took another hit from that flask. Unless we got down to business, the brandy wasn't gonna last. But I could call room service and charge it to Narbonne. When he heard I'd made contact, he'd swallow a six-hundred-buck champagne bill without his eyes even watering.

Jacobs tilted his glass and studied the amber liquid inside like he was reading his fortune there.

—Your Agency believes we have a wet operation in progress against elderly leaders of Rightist circles.

—Cut the shit. They think you got a rhythm going—and the last big beat is causing an international incident by taking out former President Reagan.

Jacobs looked surprised, maybe even shaken.

—How can they believe that? With the present political situation, the reforms in the Soviet Union. . . .

—Look, man, you guys got a mixed track record. Today, it's clean up the act. Next week, all the act-cleaners could be on trial for selling out the Revolution—and confessing to it.

When he shrugged, he looked a little like Narbonne. But then Blue Section is a bureaucracy, too.

—Captain, I am here to give you a message.

—Cut the shit. You killed Wren. I saw you in your limo. That's why you had one of your killers using me for target practice at the beach, isn't it?

Jacobs pretended surprise. —I assure you neither I nor any of my people was responsible for either act.

—I suppose you were just hanging out in the Athena parking lot looking for a cute boy.

—I had received word I might find a . . . former associate at Athena's. Instead I saw you . . . and I remembered East Berlin.

—I'm surprised you recognized me.

—One remembers another who has pointed a machine gun at him. Machine guns concentrate the mind, whet the recollections.

—Yeah, well, your people made a serious mistake in East Berlin.

—And you acted reasonably. You exacted only necessary violence. That's why I'm here. I was assigned to make my communication when and to whom I saw fit. I know you to be a reasonable man.

—There aren't many who'd agree with that. Okay, you're here. What have you got to say?

—First, let me say, I am authorized to speak by the highest levels of my government. . . .

—You mean the State Security Ministry?

—I mean exactly what I said.

—Ah . . .

—Please assure your people that we have no such operation in progress nor are we contemplating any such operation. It is unthinkable.

—Why aren't your folks talking to my folks officially?

—That would be imprudent. Officially, we have no knowledge of, nor interest in, what must be called internal criminal acts in the United States. Even back channels would be too sensitive. Back channels become front channels when the issue possesses . . . magnitude.

Jacobs seemed at ease. For all you could tell, he was in his own country, his own hotel room. I was the one who'd busted in to pass the time of day—or night, whatever it was outside.

—One thing more. Whatever this business is about, it is a rogue operation.

—If you say who, we could get this behind us.

—If . . . no, *when* I know, you will know.

—Any ideas?

—I think . . . it is not political. If it were political, I would already know.

That got me quiet. If the crazy string of murders that had caught Camille up in it wasn't political, what the hell was it?

—The woman who died on Hollywood Boulevard, Jacobs asked in a quiet voice, —was it the woman you came into the Democratic Republic to free?

—No, I said. —She's still around. It was . . . another woman.

—Ah, he nodded. —I've thought of what you said as you left the apartment building. It still puzzles me, but then I'm not an authority on bourgeoisie ideation.

—There you go, I told him. —We all got something to learn.

Jacobs got up, poured the last of his flask into my glass and held out his hand a little awkwardly. I took it. Why not? Who says he couldn't have gotten through to the *Volkspolizei* at the border before Candy and me made it across?

—Perhaps we will do business again.

—How do I reach you? You're not listed at the consulate. . . .

—No. I neglected to provide myself with a visa. Travel is so complex nowadays. If it is necessary, I'll reach you.

He was in the hall as I called out to him.

—How did you get in the country? Did they push you into a diplomatic pouch with an air supply?

He laughed as if he couldn't believe I'd asked.

—I walked across the border, he said with a deep laugh. —Near Tijuana. Isn't that how everyone comes in?

When he was gone, I checked my watch. It was 5 A.M., and

outside it was still dark. Back home, people would be at work, but I had an hour or two more of sleep coming and I expected I was gonna need it.

Jacobs hadn't solved anything. He'd just opened up the game. Or had he? If he wanted to put a slider past us, wouldn't I be the best batter to throw it to? I pulled the sheet and a blanket or two over me then, and, without trying to work that question through, I fell asleep. Without a single dream.

When Candy's call came through, I was over being tired. Exhaustion was replaced with an appetite I couldn't believe. I needed three or four slices of Georgia country ham, half a dozen eggs, and a heap of grits poured over with butter. Biscuits would be nice, but toast soaked in red-eye gravy would do. Never mind. I wasn't gonna get any of it. Not in L.A. They probably had guacamole on zwieback for breakfast.

—Yeah, what? I asked her.

—Meet me at the bookshop. I want to show Daddy the film. He might recognize someone in the crowd.

—I thought you were gonna give it to Narbonne.

—I had second thoughts. Before we go to Narbonne, I want to cover every bet. If I'm going to get straight with those people, I don't want Al picking up on something I missed.

It was politics, not investigation, but then you don't get ahead in the Agencies doing the work. You get ahead by covering your own ass and busting the other guy's. Anyhow, it seemed that Candy had an interesting political streak, courtesy of her old man. So why not see where it went.

Outside, the sun shone down the way it almost always does. Hollywood Boulevard was coming to life—if you can call it that. Now I looked at it, it wasn't much different from the French Quarter back home except for the width of the streets: T-shirt shops, hamburger dumps, Asian collectibles, falafel stands, a high-class army-surplus store, old-time movie houses with foreign architectural motifs that looked kind of lonesome and silly shoved in between a tobacco shop and an eat-on-the-run burrito joint.

Old man Hebron was just opening the doors of the book shop as I parked out front. He smiled and gave me a ceremonious handshake.

—Candace is on the way. She explained about the film. She's bringing a projector.

We went inside, back to his living quarters. There was an espresso machine I hadn't noticed before, and it was puffing away. I already felt better. The old man poured two cups and dropped slivers of lemon peel into them.

As he did I spotted an untidy pile of paper-covered mimeographed scripts stacked on one of the bookshelves. I picked up the top one: APPOINTMENT IN MUNICH. A SCREENPLAY BY MILTON HEBRON. It was dated 1934, and had the old MGM logo on it.

—Damn. You were writing movies before I was born.

He sort of smiled sadly as he gave me the espresso.

—In those days, we thought we were going to win the world and make it better . . .

—Yeah, don't we all.

—. . . but it went to hell in Spain, and afterward nothing was right again.

—You got to forgive me, Mr. Hebron. I don't know much about those old times. We were having our own old times down South.

He smiled and nodded.

—They don't talk about the war down there, do they?

—Sure. Only it's still the Confederate War. Or maybe the Second World War. Louisiana didn't send too many boys to Spain.

—Except for Phil Stern, maybe I wouldn't have gotten involved, either.

—Phil Stern?

—My best friend. He was an actor, a very fine actor. But beyond that, he was a deeply committed political person. We grew up next-door neighbors in Brooklyn. We joined the International Brigade together. His death was a great tragedy.

—Got himself killed doing duty for the Spanish, huh?

Hebron shook his head.

—No, he came home. They killed him here.

I was about to say something, but the old man cut me off.

—No, no, that's political rhetoric. Phil . . . killed himself.

—Umm. Got ashamed of what he'd done?

I hit the wrong key with that one. Hebron stared at me coldly. I hadn't meant to come down on the old man like that, but I don't take to being bullshitted, and it was pure bullshit if he wanted me to think the Left was a bunch of nice guys fighting for freedom. I'd seen too many bodies strung on barbed wire or blown to pieces in the dead zone between East and West.

In fact, it had gotten so bad that me and some buddies had gotten involved in private action. One summer, moving from one deserted building to another along the border, we'd popped more than a dozen Vopos—using their own ammunition on them. For a while, it had got where nobody East raised their heads out of the watch towers to see if some poor bastard was trying to make it across to our side. Show your head and you might get a 7.65 between the eyes. It crossed my mind to ask Jacobs how he enjoyed that summer—that is, if I ever saw him again.

—No, Captain Trapp. HUAC demanded Phil betray his friends and his principles. And he found it . . . more convenient to die.

—Candy's momma was rapping with us about the HUAC

hearings yesterday. Seems they gave a lot of you people a hard time.

The old man sat there with his empty espresso cup in his hands, remembering.

—It started in 1947. All of a sudden, the pro-Soviet movies we'd made during the war were . . . subversive. By 1951, if you'd ever been a Party member, written in favor of the Popular Front, supported the revolution . . . You had to take a loyalty oath to be in the Writers Guild or Screen Actors Guild. Reagan was president of SAG then. He'd been a liberal. Then he saw the light. Like a lot of people. Like his buddy Will Mohr.

—Will Mohr, I repeated. I recognized the name as the first one on the list of Reagan's friends who'd recently departed under suspicious circumstances.

—A lousy B actor. He got in tight with the Committee. He named everybody he knew. Because of Mohr, Nat Wren came around to put pressure on me. I told him to screw himself. Two days later, they subpoenaed me. My guts froze. I called Phil. He was an important star in those days. He had the lead in my last film.

—*Under the Double Eagle?*

Hebron looked surprised.

—That's right. How did you know?

—Candy's momma mentioned it.

—I wanted to warn Phil. He was always being asked to act in European films. I thought if he left the country for a while, the craziness might blow over. But it was no good. He'd been subpoenaed, too.

—So they made you testify?

—Two days. I learned all about Gehenna. . . .

—Huh?

—Hell. They asked me a question, and I refused to answer. They asked another, I refused again. Then they asked the first, and I said I didn't know or couldn't say. They asked me if I was still a member of the Party. I'd never been a member of the Party. I tried to say that, but they cut me off. That bastard Bearden named a dozen battles in the Spanish War, asking if I'd been there. No, I said. I was somewhere else that day.

—Who was Bearden?

—A congressman, chairman of the subcommittee on subversion in films. They had these files. . . . They knew everything, everything.

Hebron got quiet then. His eyes were wide and full of fear staring out into his patio as if the Committee were seated there with a brand-new bunch of questions for him. I wondered if that's how he'd looked forty years before when the whole weight of the U.S. Congress had come down on him.

I was fixing to ask a few more questions when Candy walked in with a projector and the film. She sensed the tension in her father and gave him a quizzical look as she set up the machine.

—Sorry to start our day off like this, Daddy. I wouldn't ask you to do this if it weren't real important to both Rat and me.

The old man nodded without looking up.

I lit a Marsh-Wheeling cigar and walked outside on Fairfax Avenue while Candy ran the film for her daddy. I wasn't gonna see anything in it I hadn't seen before, and I'd seen enough of that. Reminded me of some lines from a poem:

> *I knew a girl saw* Gone with the Wind
> *in half a dozen towns.*
> *She said it was the South*
> *lost every time.*

It was time to put my mind on business and stop licking my wounds. I'd pushed Narbonne into giving me a job, and I liked to earn my money. What did I know just now? And what did it mean?

Was Jacobs trying to snow me—or was he paying back an old favor? Forget that. In Marxism, you got no friends, no favors. The East Bloc thinks a lot like the mob. The Party is their Thing. But why would Jacobs look me up to mess with my head? Maybe because he knew I'd seen him? Maybe because once before I'd come looking for him and found him.

Candy come out and beckoned me back inside.

The old man looked pale. —What a terrible film, Hebron said to me. —It must be very painful for you to see. Where did you ever find it?

—An Italian company, di Silva Productions, just happened to be filming the ceremony. Did you see anyone you know?

—I'm sorry, Hebron said, spreading his hands. —Only Wren. It's amazing how little he'd changed.

—Nobody else? Candy pressed. —No old Leftist crony from the HUAC days?

Hebron looked at his daughter. —I wish Elaine hadn't told you about that.

—I'm sure it's all in your file at the Agency. I just never asked to see it. I never suspected my father. . . .

Candy stopped, and began packing up her projector and sticking wires and the film in her purse. Now it would go to the Agencies, and they'd spend a couple of hundred man-hours looking for some Russian geek hanging around the edge of the crowd on Hollywood Boulevard to see his work go down. And they'd think they saw somebody, only it wouldn't be anybody, and they'd run it again and again. God knows how many times Camille would jerk and twitch her life away on film for a government audience.

I shook hands with Milton Hebron.

—Thanks for your time, I said. —And the history lesson.

He shook his head. Then he reached over into that bookcase where he kept his old scripts and pulled out a dog-eared leather binder and handed it to me. THE SELL-OUT, a faded paper label on the front read, and just below, it said A SCREENPLAY BY MILTON HEBRON.

—I'd like you to have this, Captain Trapp. This was written later. After they ruined me, killed Phil Stern, sent the survivors into exile. If you have a little time, read it. Maybe it'll help you understand.

Candy phoned Narbonne from her car while I stowed the projector in the trunk of the BMW. Sure she had a car phone. In California, they got phones everywhere. At the Hollywood Roosevelt, they've got phones in the bathrooms. Next to the toilets. See, in L.A. they live by the Deal. Never mind what follows: the real art form is the Deal. You never know when a Deal is going down. How would you like to lose the Big One because you were in the can? As to placing the phone next to the crapper, maybe that's got something to do with the substance of the Deal.

Candy told Narbonne we had the film. We should take a meeting. Take? That's what they say. Narbonne told her he was just leaving for lunch, and named a place. She hung up, whipped the BMW around, and pointed it toward what they like to call the heart of Hollywood.

As we drove I looked through the old script her father had given me.

Candy paused at a red light and glanced over at me.

—Why are you wasting time reading that?

I silently handed her the script and pointed at the cast of characters.

—Will Mohr, Harold Swanson, Abe Peretz, Louis Werner,

Nat Wren . . . , she read. She suddenly looked like she'd just seen the start of World War Three out of the corner of her eye.

—Oh, my God, she whispered. —Reagan's dead friends . . . they're all listed as characters in . . . my father's screenplay.

—You mean to tell Narbonne about the script? I asked Candy as we tooled east on Sunset.

She bit her lip and said nothing. I didn't blame her. She was already on the spot because of her old man's Leftist connections. If it turned out that he had a clear grudge against every one of the victims, that wasn't gonna get Candy a promotion and a raise.

I put my head back against the leather rest and closed my eyes. It was time to sort stuff out into mental packages, then drop it into the hole in my mind where the real work gets done. Even Hebron's script and the long, sad story that went with it didn't impress me too much. He had all the motive in the world, but Mohr and Wren and the rest of them hadn't been taken down by an old man who spent his days now reading the Talmud.

—I guess I have to, she finally answered.

—Take my advice and don't do it, I said. —Let it ride.

She looked surprised, then unhappy.

—Rat, you can't cover this thing for me. If my father's involved in this, better I bring it out. If the Agency finds out I knew something and kept quiet, they'd think I was in bed with him and his old Leftist friends.

—You want to be voted Miss All-American, or get down on these killings?

—Don't talk to me like that.

—Don't you bullshit me, girl. Bullshit is for bedtime.

She flushed and went silent again. I let her cook for a minute, then: —I'm just saying you and me ought to check out the HUAC connection without bringing in the whole fucking bureaucracy.

—All right. But how can we keep Al off our back while we do that?

—That's easy. I'll just tell him I talked to Jacobs.

She almost ran into a car alongside us.

We walked in through the back door of a place called Musso and Frank's Grill. The oldest restaurant in Hollywood, the sign said. Since 1919. I didn't laugh, but I couldn't help thinking of Antoine's in New Orleans. Since 1847—and in the same family, the Alciatores and the Gustes, since the day it opened.

Narbonne had a booth in a corner near the back. The place was already filling up and the noise level was rising. We slipped in across from him while he practiced upper-level-management style with a menu. He started talking without looking up.

—Where's the film?

Candy slid it across to him.

—Who's seen it?

She said we had. Good. I'd meant to tell her not to mention her family.

—I'll courier it to Washington after we make a copy.

—Save your money . . . oops, *my* money, I said. —It's just Nat Wren fixing to talk, and a lady being electrocuted.

Narbonne did his government shrug as he pocketed the film. Then he turned his attention back to the menu.

—Try the fried scallops, he said to me.

—They got a lot of nice things in here. Braised short ribs, sauerbraten. . . .

Narbonne looked at me like I was a trial to him.

—How was the corned beef at Nate 'n Al's?

—Outstanding. Grade-A number one dead in there.

—You want the scallops.

—Man, how are you so damned sure?

—Remember the oysters en brochette at Galatoire's?

—Do I remember my momma?

A waiter in a nice red jacket turned up about then.

—Gimme the fried scallops, I said.

—Same, Narbonne told him.

—Sand dabs, cooked well, Candy finished up.

—And give me a Guinness and a Heineken and one glass, I added.

That was an old habit of mine I'd picked up around the military bases in Europe. The two beers you could count on were Guinness and Heineken.

The waiter cleared out, and Narbonne pointed at the bread.

—Remember the bread at Arnaud's in the old days, before the family sold it?

—Ummm.

—This is better, sourdough French.

It was. It was as good as the fresh French at Bill Long's bakery out on Freret Street years ago. I pasted butter on it and looked around the place. Dark wood paneling on the booths, high ceilings, quiet service. I could see why Narbonne liked to take his lunch out of the office. If I was working out here, I'd hang out for the atmosphere alone. We'd see about the food.

All right, I thought. It's about that time. I kind of gave Candy a look out of the corner of my eye.

—You paying for this, Alphonse?

—Yes, goddammit, I'm paying.

—Good. I'm glad you said that. I got two pieces of news for you.

—All right.

—Jacobs dropped by the Roosevelt and woke me up this morning.

Narbonne looked at me like I'd said Jesus was on his way back.

—That's impossible.

—Okay, I didn't know that. I guess it was some other KGB type. But whoever it was gave me a message for you.

I told him what I'd been told to tell him. All the words, the nuances, the expressions. I'm good at that kind of thing. You testify at as many homicide trials as I do, you get very precise. You get approximate with a good defense attorney, he'll pull off your gold badge and jam it up your ass.

Narbonne shook his head. For just a minute, he lost that smart-assed superior look he liked to lay out on the world.

—A rogue . . . operation, he said slowly. —I wonder if it's true.

I gave him one of his own shrugs.

—Why bother telling me if it's not?

—Disinformation, he said tensely. —Isn't that your reading, Candace?

Candy nodded like a fool. I wanted to whip her. She's a better woman than that. But I just grinned back at him.

—Naw, I said. —Jacobs didn't need to come by spreading disinformation. You guys do that to yourselves.

—You're one of us guys now, Narbonne said in a nasty tone.

—Right, I am. Shit, maybe I'm even disinformed.

Narbonne started to drag himself out of the booth.

—I've got to get people on Jacobs.

—Goddammit, Alphonse, what do you say we eat first, okay?

He looked at me like I was an enemy agent. Hell, maybe I was. If I had had to pick sides right then, I'd have asked who was gonna let me finish my lunch.

—I don't think you quite grasp what you've stumbled across, Trapp. . . .

I motioned him back into the booth.

—I've got something else. It's not international and all that shit, but it's interesting.

He sat down like a nervous school kid who needed to hit the can but don't dare raise his hand.

—Did you folks happen to notice that every one of the old men who's bit it had something to do with the House Un-American Activities Committee investigations out here back in the forties and fifties?

I heard Candy draw in her breath. She probably thought I was fixing to roll over on her. Maybe it slipped her mind that I was on temporary assignment. I wasn't bucking for GS-21. Narbonne stared at me like he didn't know me.

—Is that so?

—Yeah, it's so.

He thought for a moment.

—All right. But so what?

—Those were rocky times. A lot of people got hurt.

—The way I've heard it, the ones who got hurt deserved it.

—Yeah, well, that may be true. But deserving it don't make a poke in the eye sit any better, does it?

—Anyhow, who the hell remembers back that far?

I laughed. Al had been away from New Orleans and in government service way too long. His historical epochs were four years long. Every time the country got a new administration, time stopped and started all over again. I was gonna make a comment on that, but the waiter beat me to it.

Once he got into his fried scallops and shoestring potatoes,

Al kind of cooled out. When I started on mine, I could see why. Short of DEFCON 4, you tend to finish your lunch at Musso's before heading out to battle. What can I tell you? Narbonne didn't know jack-shit about police work, but he sure had a tongue in his head.

We ate without saying anything. Life is too short to talk when you got a fine meal in front of you.

Finally, Narbonne looked across at me as he put down the last of his scallops.

—I've been thinking about the House Un-American Activities Committee thing . . . you really think it goes anywhere?

—Man, what do I know? You guys are into geopolitics and all that crap. Me? I'm just a cop. I go where the leads take me.

Narbonne nodded.

—The Service doesn't think that way . . .

—You got to convince me they think at all.

—. . . but maybe *you* ought to nose around, Narbonne finished, ignoring my remark.

I gave him this big fond smile. I was hoping he'd say that, believing he'd say that. See, I knew his mind.

—Can I keep this lady with me? I asked.

He studied Candy like he was doping out the odds she was on the other side. Then he nodded again.

—Sure. That makes sense. That kind of angle is why she's on the case. Stay together and check in with me if you find anything worth moving on.

He looked at his watch and waved to the waiter for the check.

—There's a meeting downtown in forty minutes. I've got to get out of here.

He tossed the waiter his gold card and drummed his fingers on the table while he waited. I loved that he was writing us off and out of the investigation. He'd gotten the film and heard about Jacobs dropping by my room. The way he saw it, Candy and I were people he didn't need anymore. Now he was going to his boss and tell him that the KGB was mounting this terrible plot, and they had to use all their resources to find Jacobs. Shit, I could start out at the Thrifty Drug Store on Fountain Avenue and find him before they did.

Narbonne scrawled his name and a small tip on the credit card invoice and slid out of the booth.

—Catch you later, he said, as he pulled on his sunglasses and headed out the back to the parking lot. Candy looked a little confused.

—What are we supposed to do now? she asked me.

—That's easy. Who's left in that cast of characters? Who's still alive that had anything to do with the Committee hearings your daddy wrote about?

Candy pulled the script from the big leather pouch she used for a purse and checked the front page.

—There's Ronald Reagan, she said. —He was president of the Screen Actors Guild back then.

—Now you sound like Narbonne. Who else?

—Congressman Thomas Bearden of California.

—Yeah, your daddy mentioned him to me. He was the HUAC head honcho back then, wasn't he?

—He chaired the subcommittee that came to Hollywood.

—Is he still alive?

—I can find out.

I ordered another Guinness and Heineken while she was on the phone in back, talking to the Agency. I liked this place. When we got done what we had to do, and before I flew home, I was gonna do myself another breakfast at Nate 'n Al's and a supper right here. Maybe I'd try the braised spareribs. Finding a good restaurant in a strange town is like finding an oasis in the desert. Makes you feel more secure.

Candy slipped back into the booth beside me.

—Bearden's alive but deep into his eighties.

—Retirement home?

—Nope. Has a ranch in the Santa Monica Mountains near Kanan Road.

—Honey, don't talk hieroglyphics to me. Where can we find the man?

—It's out the Ventura Freeway about thirty-five miles.

—What do you say we hit it, girl?

—You don't just walk in on a retired congressman, Rat.

—Right. I see that, and I don't especially want to, lover. But much is forgiven when you turn up unexpectedly saving some politician's ass.

When you hit Calabasas driving out the Ventura Freeway, you're in the Santa Monica Mountains. They're not the Rockies. They're not even the Smokies, but they've got their own kind of hold on things.

The hills are smooth rock-studded mounds. Some are no more than rising grassy slopes. But here and there you see stands of Pacific oak and pepper trees and eucalyptus moving in the breeze along ridges and down into valleys where even in early afternoon the shadows have begun to spread out.

Candy drove, and I looked. I guess she knew all that country, because it didn't seem to do a thing for her. Me? I loved it. See, I was meant to be a country boy. Coming into the world in New Orleans, growing up in the projects was some kind of glitch in the plan. I thought about how it would be to own this kind of soft, flowing tan and brown and gray land, how it would be to wake up in a chill dawn and see if you could do your jogging up and down those hills.

I was supposed to be thinking about all that Un-American Activities crap, but as we turned onto Kanan Road and kept going higher, I couldn't focus my attention.

The Southern California land is Louisiana turned inside out. Back home, things teem, grow over and under and around everything. Wisteria, honeysuckle, morning glory, moon flowers, palmetto, all kind of swamp and marsh bushes struggling against one another for a piece of ground and a little sunlight.

They call Southern California "semi-arid." What that means is that everything that grows there fights for water. The land is gaunt and tan, the rocks look like hardened mud. But the grass and flowers and trees that win the struggle—find a drop of moisture—are something to behold.

We turned off Kanan Road onto Mulholland Highway as the shadows grew and the hot afternoon started to turn cool.

—That's the place, Candy said, pointing at a gate along the dusty road.

—Where? I don't see nothing but hills and . . . what's that stuff?

—Chaparral, she said with a smile. —The house must be in the valley, down that road behind the gate. We'll have to use the intercom.

She pointed to a call box on a post near the high iron gate.

—No, I said, —that's not gonna get it. If the old man don't wanna see us, all he has to do is hang up. I'd rather he has to slam the door.

Candy wasn't convinced.

—This isn't New Orleans. You can't crash through the gate, Rat. People have a right to privacy.

I did my best to look hurt.

—Honey, you got the wrong idea about me. What do you say we crawl over the wood fence and play like we're lost and looking for directions? We leave the gate standing, and just screw around with Bearden's privacy a little bit?

She parked the car on the side of the road. —I'm going to be sorry I did this, she said.

—Then stay here, honey. All I'm gonna do is ask the old gentleman a few questions.

—No, I want to hear the answers, too.

—That all there is to it?

Candy gave me a funny look, then smiled and reached over for my hand.

—My God, Rat, you do read me. It's like having you inside my . . .

—I been there, too, I laughed as we got out of the car. It didn't take any kind of genius to know that Candy wanted a look at the man who had driven her father out of the movie business and into the ground.

We were over the fence and down the road then, with me wondering why anybody would build a great big gate, with an intercom and electric controls, when all they got is an ordinary rail fence around the property. I decided Californians are big for front. You show 'em a lavish gate and all that electronic shit out front, and they'll let the rest go on by. That's all right. We got people like that back home in New Orleans. Take a run by Audubon Place off St. Charles next time you go down for Mardi Gras.

A hundred yards down the road, we were into a valley and could feel that California chill creeping up around us. Candy said we were just a few miles away from the Pacific. Maybe that accounted for it, but as we walked down and made a turn, it felt like my suit jacket wasn't gonna be enough.

On the right, there was a big pasture deep in grass and wild oats. Here and there, a boulder stood out of the ground. Horses were cropping at the grass. They raised their heads and stared as we walked by.

Then the house seemed to rear up in front of us. It was a big frame place, colored brown and tan so that it seemed to have grown out of the dry earth instead of being built. There was chaparral and eucalyptus trees around it, a few oaks and magnolias standing off a little. On each side, a ravine cut through the tan rocks and scruffy grass. One of them was filled with water forming a pond right below the house. I wondered if the old man kept fish in it.

In the driveway, parked headed toward us, was another one of them big black limos.

We were maybe a hundred feet from the front door when someone in the house took a shot at us. I heard the report and an angry snarl, like a hornet perched on your ear, as the bullet ricocheted off a rock close by.

I pulled Candy to the ground off the road and rolled into some brush on the edge of the ravine.

—Maybe we *should* have used the intercom, she said flatly without looking at me.

—Folks usually go to shooting when you trespass a little out here?

—God, who knows anymore? After that animal Manson and all the other freaks . . .

—Say, I called out. —We just need some directions. No harm meant.

No answer. We could have been in that little valley all by ourselves for all the noise there was.

—Okay, I told Candy. —I don't know what's going down. Maybe the old man's nuts. Maybe not. But I'm going in. You packing?

Candy pulled a Browning 9mm autoload out of her purse.

—What do you want me to do?

—I'm gonna flank him, see if I can't get inside and explain we didn't mean any trouble. If he comes out the front, stop him. Tell him he's under arrest for assault on a federal officer.

—But if you go inside . . .

—Honey, I'm on an investigation.

—You didn't identify yourself.

—Yeah? Who's gonna back him up if he says that?

I left Candy shaking her head and sliding a round into her pistol and moved down to the edge of the pond below the house on the left. The shadows were deepening and the slanted ground was covered with mimosas and chaparral, and Bearden was gonna have to have good eyesight and fast reflexes to hit me. Near the rear of the house, there was a dam stopping the water as the land fell away behind. I kept my eyes on the windows of the house. They were all closed and dark. As I moved past the dam and began inching my way up on the house, I was starting to wonder if it was the old man who'd taken the shot at us. I knew a few congressmen from Louisiana. They never shot at people. Shit, they might hit a constituent—or somebody they could beg a buck from.

What if my hunch was right, and the killers had beaten us to him? Then I stopped under a tall magnolia and started putting my mental house in order. Wandering around on a beautiful piece of land was messing me up, making me forget that this was still police work. That problem never came up in New Orleans. You know that place is dangerous. You can see it and smell it and feel it.

The back of the house was a series of decks that looked out over a pasture and a stand of oak trees way out toward the rear of the property. Between where I was standing and the house itself, the ground was open and rising. There were a couple of levels of lawn and garden up there before you reached the house, but no cover at all taller than a rose bush. If anybody was watching, I was gonna be a prime target when I started across that open ground. Maybe nobody was watching at all. Whoever had taken the shot at us might still be in front. And maybe not.

No need to stand around under a tree with my pistol in my pocket and my gun in my hand. I ran up over the lawn and ducked behind some low bushes, listening for any sound that might tip me off. Then I saw some kind of structure over to my left. It looked like a wine barrel lying on its side. Some wine barrel. It was ten feet long and maybe seven feet wide. There was a door with a pane of glass in it at the end facing me. Reckon old man Bearden had him a smokehouse? Anyhow, it was a piece of cover, the last piece except for some bushes before I hit the back deck of the place.

I thought I heard something as I ran to the wine barrel, but I made it clean and paused. I looked out around the side, up to the deck with its wooden railing. The windows behind were dark. I was just thinking about making a run for the back deck when I heard the sound of metal against metal and hit the ground.

Turned out that was a good idea. Because when the shooting started, it wasn't a single-shot rifle or even a semiautomatic. Somebody up on one of those decks had himself a full-auto assault rifle, and he was emptying the clip. At the wine barrel.

The wine barrel rocked and shook at the impact of the bullets, and I wondered if the bastard up on the deck had in mind to roll it over me. If the shots hadn't been going through the wood like it was Swiss cheese, he might have brought that off.

The shooting stopped for a moment. The shooter was reloading. In the silence, I could hear the wine barrel groaning and settling. A slat on it fell in. I decided that it was time to move on—even though I had no idea what lay up the terraces ahead of me.

I was up and moving before the clown with the machine gun could get back into business. Up ahead, the terrace was supported by a low stone wall. The stones didn't sit more then three feet off the ground, but I reckoned I could settle for that.

I rolled into the rocks and wiggled like a snake up to near the end of the wall. For the first time since Candy and I had gone over the fence back at the road, I had me a little advantage. I pulled my .357 and cocked it.

I saw that there was another deck above the first one, off the second floor of the house. I squinted and tried to see muzzle flash as Machine Gun Man began working at blasting down the wall about ten feet behind me. When I saw it, it wasn't much, but it was enough.

I placed my first AP round two feet and a little more behind the flash. Then I fired twice more. One wad-cutter and another AP.

The shooting stopped. Somebody up there moaned and then went to screaming. It was the sweetest sound I'd heard since the last time a woman told me she loved me.

I didn't wait for a formal surrender. I was up and running toward that lower deck, reloading as I ran. I come up the stairs and slammed into the wall of the house between what looked like a kitchen and some French doors that went into the living room.

—*Jesus Christo,* I heard somebody moan from above. Then he went to yelling in what sounded like Spanish, and somebody else answered him. I'd have given my annual salary for a thirty-second Berlitz course just then. But on the other hand, whatever they were saying, I knew there were two of them, and I had only chopped down one.

The kitchen door was open, standing ajar. I ran into a cooking island in the middle of the room and ducked behind it. Then I pushed open a door across the way and found myself at the foot of stairs leading to the second floor. But I was hearing running footsteps from my left, past a door that looked like it led into the living room. I hit the floor and knocked open a slatted dark-wood door as I rolled on past. The room in there was in shadows, but I could see light coming from a hallway across the living room.

I ran over a magazine rack without losing my balance and checked out the hall. One door opened into a study, another into a garage. A Buick sedan and a tractor were parked there. Then the automatic door opener hummed, and the garage door raised slowly. I scanned the opening with my Magnum.

He was out and firing a pistol at me by the time I saw him. I shot and maybe popped him, but the adrenalin was cooking in his brain, and he opened the door of the limo and had it started as I emptied my piece into the trunk, hoping to open the gas tank. As the limo spun its tires, starting up the long inclined driveway toward Mulholland Highway, I was standing there with my thumb in my butt and an empty pistol I knew I couldn't load quick enough to take another shot—and knowing I didn't dare shoot anyhow because I had no idea where Candy was.

Then, as the car fishtailed over the asphalt, I found out where she was. I heard that Browning of hers crackling over and over again. But it didn't seem to have any effect, and the limo rushed up the long drive and beyond my seeing.

I reloaded anyway and waited for Candy to walk up to the house, motioning her to run. We still had the second floor of the house to check out. And old man Bearden to find.

She was breathless and pale when she reached the garage.

—Goddammit, the thing was armor-plated, she choked out. —I could see my rounds bouncing. Even the windows were bulletproof.

—Yeah, well, I keep learning stuff about your hometown here. Nobody told me the movie business was so dangerous.

—Did you find Bearden?

—Hell, I never got a chance to look. Come on.

We went inside, covering one another as we went up the

stairs to a long hallway smelling of gunpowder, with wisps of smoke hanging in the unmoving air. Candy checked out a couple of bedrooms while I went over a porch that overlooked the front driveway. As I opened the door a north wind blew in, scattering the smoke, thinning the odor. At the end of the hallway, there was one more room.

—Whatever there is, it's got to be inside, Candy said.

I nodded and hit the door shoulder-first, rolling inside with my Magnum up and ready. I could have saved myself a set of sore muscles. The room was quiet.

My eyes moved past a desk, a night table, a bed, to French doors opening onto a balcony. Some of the panes of glass were shattered, and I could see somebody slumped against the wooden rails out there.

—Cover, I called back to Candy, and moved to the balcony.

When I pulled his head up and took a look at his face, I had this funny jolt. I'd seen him before. He was the sunrise shooter who had followed Candy and me out to the beach and pumped a magazine into a sand dune. He looked like he could have been from New Orleans—dark, curly hair, thick brows—and a Magnum wad-cutter right through the middle of his chest. There was another shot through his leg, and he'd soaked the wooden floor of the balcony with his blood. This had to be the one singing out to Jesus in Spanish as he felt his life going off on him. Sonofabitch calling on Jesus right after he tried to kill me. I turned loose his hair and dropped his face back to the deck.

Next to him was just what I'd expected to find. An AK-47-m with a short barrel, and an empty magazine next to it. The wooden stock was shattered, and that made three hits with six shots. All right, I thought, wondering how it must feel to hold the high ground and all the edge and still get your ass shot off.

—Rat . . .

I turned and squinted back into the dimly lit room. Candy was standing over the bed.

—I think I've found . . . the congressman.

She had. He was just a fragile, worn-out old man lying in his pajamas like he was asleep, except his eyes were open and staring up at us like the last thing he'd seen in this world was the living image of his worst nightmare. I expected maybe he had.

I looked him over while Candy stood there like she'd been dropped into liquid nitrogen. There wasn't a mark on his body. The Spaniards or whoever they were had done a good job. If we hadn't turned up, a housekeeper or friend would have found him, and the medics would have written him up as a stroke. How they'd sent him on, I couldn't tell. Maybe smothering, maybe an injection. Forensics would work that out now that we knew it wasn't anything close to natural causes.

While I looked for needle marks and such, Candy loosened up and picked up the phone on the old man's desk. She didn't call the L.A. County Sheriff's office. She called Narbonne. As she whispered into the phone I couldn't figure whether she was doing politics or trying to keep this last killing close. It didn't really matter, did it? Because we had one dead shooter out on the balcony—but the other one had gotten clear. By now, whoever had thought this whole scheme up knew that he'd scored again. I hated that, because as far as I could remember, the old man lying over there dead in his bed was the last name on anybody's list—except for maybe Ronald Reagan's.

12

Candy had called Narbonne, and Narbonne seemed to have called everybody in Southern California and a few Washington types I hadn't seen yet. They went over the place for hours. It was dark before they finished stripping Bearden's files, rifling his desk, and studying the dead shooter like something in his pockets or the threads of his blood-soaked sportshirt held the Secret of the Ages.

Then, with the county sheriff squealing like a pig, the feds started piling everything but the old man's refrigerator into unmarked vans outside. I thought the sheriff was gonna go for his gun when they wrapped up the old man and the dead hitter and packed them away in the last van.

—Goddammit to hell, this is a state crime, and you sonsofbitches haven't got a shadow of jurisdiction to just walk in here and . . .

That pudgy, sandy-haired man I'd seen at Camille's funeral, the one who looked like an anchorman for a tank-town TV news show, took the sheriff by the arm and moved him over by the balcony. I got just close enough to hear Old Sandy say that this was a federal investigation of a possible assassination conspiracy, and that the U.S. Code covered what the Secret Service and everybody else was doing. Did the sheriff want to go talk it over with a federal magistrate?

The sheriff reckoned not. The last damned thing in the world a local official wants to get involved in is an assassination investigation. I had an old buddy who was working in Dallas in November of 1963. He said by the time it was over, the paperwork in his office alone weighed one hundred and seventy-five pounds.

The sheriff followed the vans to the gate, where we'd heard a horde of press types were waiting to interview any warm body that left the Bearden ranch. They'd pounce on him like hungry wolves. The murder of a prominent ex-congressman was news. Narbonne had so far been able to quash publicity about the string of killings, but he was gonna have trouble keeping the lid on the investigation now.

He finished talking real intensely with one of his flunkies, then Narbonne beckoned Candy and me out onto the porch and the grilling started.

—Basically, you just broke in here, right?

—Basically, I said, grinning from ear to ear, —these two geeks started shooting at us. So, fundamentally, I figured to find out why, and, essentially, I killed hell out of the one with the Kalashnikov. You got a problem with that?

Narbonne just stared at us. His problem was that he hadn't been along to grab a piece of what went down.

—I've got a problem with you, Trapp. You're undisciplined. You make up your own rules. . . .

—Aw, Alphonse, you been talking to the bureaucrats at N.O.P.D., huh?

Narbonne knew me. He reckoned he wasn't gonna get anything but smart-mouth out of me because his government folks weren't gonna pay my pension or buck me up the ranks. So he turned to Candy and started in on her. He wanted to know every move we'd made. The girl just kept a straight face and told him what he'd already heard from me.

As Candy stonewalled Narbonne, I was watching Narbonne's flunky through a window on the porch that looked into the hallway. He'd rigged up some kind of a fax machine, plugging it into a telephone jack in the wall. He was watching it while he talked fast to someone on a separate cellular radiophone. He looked calm enough till the fax started spitting out something. Then his eyes got wide, and he couldn't hardly wait till the transmission ended. When it did, he ripped the sheets off the machine and hustled out on the porch like he had a red phone jammed up his butt.

—Chief, he interrupted Narbonne.

—What?

He handed Narbonne the sheets. I took a look over his shoulder. There was a slightly blurred photo of my shooter, only in better days, with a mean sullen expression on his face like he was the Very Baddest There Was. Next to the picture was a set of fingerprints and a block of text I couldn't make out. Narbonne set a card next to the fax sheets, and he and his dog-robber checked the prints.

—Bingo, the baby bureaucrat said with a low whistle.

Narbonne looked at Candy and me with this sober expression like, despite everything, he was gonna forgive us.

—At least you didn't kill the old man's valet or chauffeur.

—Yeah, well, that relieves us both, I told him. —You never know when a congressman's driver is gonna pack an AK-47. The way the House votes, you never know which side they're on, do you?

—Antonio Ruiz, Narbonne read off the sheet, trying to ignore me. —A stone killer. Interpol wanted him for machine-gunning to death most of a Spanish border garrison in the name of Basque liberation.

Candy looked pale. I just smiled at Narbonne. When he saw I didn't have anything to add, he shrugged.

—What can I say? You guys made a good move. It was outside procedures and against specific orders, but I'm going to forget that. . . .

See? Like trying to straighten up a hunchback. Alphonse is gonna die as dumb as he lived. They're gonna put on his tombstone, ". . . but he had good taste in food."

—Still, this confirms the Service's evaluation of the killings so far.

My grin fell like a bat off a tree limb.

—It what?

—Your big buddy Jacobs sold you a package, Trapp. This is terrorist stuff. And even if they're sending us a Spanish package, I think it was wrapped and mailed from Moscow.

Candy and I just stared at one another. I couldn't believe Narbonne was glued to that theory so tight that he had to twist and warp everything he come across to fit it.

—Al, why the hell would a fucking terrorist go gunning for an old man who hasn't been in Congress in twenty years?

That pissed him. When he frowned, his flunky frowned, too. The kid didn't know exactly why, but he frowned.

—Bearden put Ronald Reagan in the governor's mansion, Narbonne shot at me, like that closed the discussion. —The former President visits the ranch here regularly.

—Well, he wasn't here tonight. Besides, when the KGB goes wet, they don't use crazy spicks to do their work for them.

—So you've got a better theory?

—Any old theory at all beats your crap. We come out here 'cause the old man ran HUAC in L.A. He made chopped liver out of a lot of people back in the forties and fifties. All the other corpses had a hand in those hearings, too.

Narbonne looked from me to Candy and laughed. His flunky kind of sneered along. Just to keep in step.

—So a terrorist is cleaning up forty-year-old scores for a bunch of celluloid Commies—and you think that makes more sense? Narbonne walked away without waiting for an answer.

I didn't try to stop him. When he put it that way, all I had was some strong correlations—and my way of putting all the victims together wasn't any better than his. At least a plot against former President Reagan, for whatever reason, was big-time. Shit, I thought, maybe Jacobs *is* working with the Stalinists in the Kremlin.

—Rat, we have to tell Al about Daddy's script, Candy said.

—Only if you want your career ended tonight. Let's leave Al to chase his terrorists and go talk to your daddy first.

Hebron's Bookstore had a CLOSED sign up when we parked across the street. But through the glass front door we could see a light on in the back. Candy knocked. The door wasn't latched and swung open under her hand. Now Hebron's an old man and might have retired without locking his door, but given how things had been going since I entered the White Zone, I pulled my .357. Candy moved past me and walked down the aisle between the packed shelves of books toward the light.

She stopped at the door marked PRIVATE and gave a sort of stifled cry. Milton Hebron was sitting in that shabby leather chair of his, and his chest was covered with blood running down from a wound in his head. A pistol of a kind I'd never seen before was lying on the floor in front of him. A quick look said that an old man, for whatever reasons old men have, had decided to go on.

Candy called her mother, and Elaine Prescott arrived almost as soon as the police. Mrs. Precott sat with her arm around Candy, her lips tightly compressed. I couldn't tell if she was biting back tears or trying to keep words she didn't want to say from pouring out. Candy's face was ravaged, mascara running in two dark rivulets down her cheeks. I could see what she'd look like ten years older.

The shop was full of police. Lonagan, L.A.P.D.'s finest, was fooling around the old library table Hebron had used for a desk. There were battered boxes used for card files, copies of *Books in Print,* a couple of bound volumes of *Library Journal.* And right in the middle, there was an envelope on a stack of Xeroxed papers. He looked over at me.

—You always turn up when there's a death, Trapp?

—Just homicides.

—Then you shouldn't be here. This was a suicide.

Lonagan tapped the envelope. —You read this?

—Yeah.

There was nothing written on the outside of the envelope—just *Hebron's Bookstore—Judaica,* and the return address. Inside was a typed page.

Hebron had confessed to masterminding the killings, all of them: Will Mohr, Harold Swanson, Louis Werner, Abe Peretz, Nat Wren, Congressman Bearden. If you believed the note he left behind, he had hired a couple of button men to do what he couldn't do for himself. The Last Campaign, Hebron called it. Tonight, taking out Bearden, the chairman of the House subcommittee, had finished the job.

Hebron wrote that nobody had died but those who deserved to die. His victims had advanced the cause of fascism in America, had destroyed honest men in the 1940s and '50s, and had gone on to put a spiritual descendant of Francisco Franco in the White House in 1980. He'd wanted to reach Reagan, but he'd done all he could. He knew the police were close, and he'd gone through all the fascist police-state misery he intended to suffer.

The pages the note had been lying on were photocopies of

a newsletter called *The Loyalist.* I'd seen those copies delivered by Carole Klein, Hebron's lady friend, the first time I visited his shop.

A quick reading, while Lonagan wrapped up his perfunctory investigation, showed *The Loyalist* was written for and by Americans who had fought on the side of the Republic in the Spanish Civil War. Full of pointless anger and dumb hatred—the lifeblood of old men who had nothing to remember but blurred moments in a forgotten war waged a lifetime ago—and the suffering it had brought them in its wake for the rest of their lives.

When I looked up from the papers, Narbonne had come in and was studying Hebron's body like he figured to interrogate him.

Lonagan filled him in on what L.A.P.D. Forensics had turned up. The note had been typed on an old Smith-Corona typewriter Hebron kept on a table out in the bookstore area along with his invoices and orders and want-lists from customers.

The wound was consistent with having been caused by a round from that pistol, fired by the old man himself.

Powder traces were on his right hand, on his sleeve, on the fabric at the back of the chair in which he'd been sitting. If it wasn't self-inflicted, we were gonna have to prove it with exterior evidence.

The pistol was a 9mm Campo-Giro Model 1921, used in the Spanish War by officers on both sides. They'd had to look it up in a book. Nobody had ever seen one before. The thing was so old and rare, it was valuable.

—Did it belong to Hebron?

Lonagan carried it over to where Candy sat with Elaine Prescott and asked them.

—Yes, Elaine Prescott answered in clipped tones. —Milt kept it to remind him of what had happened. It's the gun his friend

Phil Stern used to kill himself. After Phil refused to testify at the HUAC hearings.

This last piece of evidence seemed to convince Narbonne. He gestured me aside.

—Damn, you tried to tell me the killings were all HUAC connected, he said, —and I didn't listen. But this does it for me. I guess you feel pretty damned proud of yourself.

—No, 'cause I think it's bullshit.

—Why?

—I can smell a crazy at fifty yards. I spent a little time with the old man. He didn't ring no bells with me.

Narbonne shrugged, dismissing my intuitions. —He was a Loyalist, fought in Spain. He spent the last forty years writing articles against our government. You telling me that's not crazy?

I didn't answer. This thing was out of hand. I didn't believe Milton Hebron had killed anybody, but what I believed and what was true just might be different things. Say Hebron hadn't set up the killings, and hadn't killed himself. Then who the hell had? Who'd added an old Leftie writer to the hit list along with all the Un-American Activities alumni?

—Hebron must have kept up some contacts with his old Spanish Commie buddies, Narbonne continued, warming to his new theory of the case. —Sure, that has to be it. So when he went looking for a gun to hire, one of them put Hebron in contact with that Basque terrorist, Ruiz.

—There was a second shooter who got away.

—Probably told Hebron what had happened to Ruiz and that he was pulling out. Or maybe that the cost was going up, and Hebron couldn't afford to complete his plan to take out Reagan, too.

It occurred to me that with that kind of quick imagination Narbonne should write spy fiction when he retired. But buy his theory or not, he was making me feel like I was playing out of my league. I had flown to California thinking I knew my job, that I could do it better than anybody. Now I had a handful of junk I couldn't sort out into any kind of pattern at all. Maybe I was just a local player. Maybe New Orleans was as much as I could handle.

Narbonne walked over to Candy and her mother.

—I'm really sorry about this, he started.

Candy nodded, thinking he meant her father's death. But I knew Narbonne better than that.

—The Agency says you should take a leave of absence.

—Thanks, but there's no need for that. I'll be all right, Candy said.

Narbonne almost had the decency to look embarrassed. —It's not optional. They want time to figure out just how much of a security threat your father really was.

—Milt was no threat to anyone, Elaine Prescott put in.

—I have six dead men who'd disagree with you, Narbonne countered. —And a dead terrorist assassin who was doing what Hebron told him to.

—So, because of my father, I'm out? My thirteen years with the Company count for nothing? Candy asked.

To no one's surprise, Narbonne shrugged without answering and moved away to talk with Lonagan.

Elaine Prescott rose abruptly to her feet, her expression stormy. —Let's go home, Candace. We need to talk about your father.

But Candy wasn't ready for that. —I have to take Rat back to his hotel.

—One of these men can do that. It's important we talk.

—We will, Mother, Candy said in a defeated voice. —But later. Then she turned away to watch silently as two coroner's assistants zipped up the body bag and carried her father's corpse out to the waiting hearse.

* * *

The Yamashira is a Japanese restaurant perched like a palace high in the Hollywood Hills. They take your car in front after you've driven a circular road up through the neighborhood below. But unless you're blind or stupid, you don't turn and go inside right off.

Candy and I stood there and looked out over the Los Angeles basin that spread out below like a treasure chest, lights from Hollywood all the way out to Palos Verdes. Candy had said she'd like a drink, and the Yamashira had drawn the job.

We sat in the bar and ordered sake, and when the delicate Japanese waitress brought it, I told her to keep the juice coming till we said stop.

—I just don't believe it, Candy said. —My father had made the great circle.

I looked at her without understanding.

—He was raised in an observing Jewish family, she went on. —His grandfather had been a Rabbi in . . . Oh, God, some place like Tiflis, I don't know. Some of his kin were Hasidic, everybody was Orthodox.

—I'm missing your point.

—After all that he'd been through, he'd . . . come back to religion. He wouldn't kill himself.

—What about the note?

—It was typed. Anybody can use a typewriter.

—What about the language? Was it the way he expressed things?

—I don't know. We weren't close. We didn't write each other a lot. Rat, I know it looks like suicide, it sounds like suicide, it feels like suicide, but . . .

Candy's arguments fueled my own suspicions. I wasn't ready to bury the old man with a suicide's epitaph just yet. Not just yet.

—The other killings seemed like something else, too. So what we've got here is a murder that was made to look like a suicide.

—But why? What motive would the people who killed all the others have to take out my father?

I thought about that as I looked out the window at the Los Angeles basin. Low clouds were whipping across the velvet darkness and beginning to obscure the patterned lines of lights below us.

—To stop us from looking any further. You saw how easy Narbonne swallowed that suicide note. He was downright anxious to believe your daddy did what it said he did.

Narbonne wanted to get things settled and put away, clear all those cases that were troubling Washington and had the Attorney General in town. See, Al wasn't handling what was going down as criminal cases to work through. He saw the whole mess as something that would help or hurt his career. That's the way you think when your life and salvation all lie inside the Beltway. I wasn't caught up in that. It didn't mean shit to me. The only stake I had in what was happening was wanting to even the score for Camille—and seeing what I could do to help Candy, especially now.

—I've got to admit Daddy was a great choice for a fall guy. But who could know that?

—Good question. Let's fool around with it awhile, I said softly. —Only someone who knew your daddy's history real well. Candy, who were your daddy's buddies?

She looked blank for a second. —Other book dealers, the people at Agudath Achim, his temple, a few old men he played chess with . . .

—Nobody else? What about that woman who publishes *The Loyalist?* The bunch that writes for it?

She wrinkled her nose. —Those people. Of course. All the old losers. The publisher is Carole Klein. . . .

—I saw her at the bookstore. Your daddy's girl friend?

—Maybe. I don't know. I think she'd be older than Daddy was. She was his agent. She used to sell his work when he was writing screenplays. They stayed in touch.

—You know where to find her?

—There's this rundown Spanish Colonial building up in the Hollywood Hills. Daddy took me there once years ago. Lots of leftovers from the thirties have offices and apartments up there. If she hasn't moved, that's where Carole lives.

—Tell you what, I said to Candy. —Why don't the two of us drop by and see that Klein lady?

13

Outside we found the night had turned raw and windy, and Candy shivered as I pushed the door to on her BMW. When I got behind the wheel, I could see tears coursing down her cheeks. Now that she was a little stoned on the sake, she was thinking of Milton Hebron, maybe realizing for the first time that the old man she'd found shot dead was the only father she was ever gonna have.

—I'm sorry. I'm just thinking that if . . . I'd tried harder with him . . .

—Done and finished, sweetheart. Put it aside and get ready for your next mistake.

She fumbled in her purse for a tissue. —What's that supposed to mean?

—I believe it means . . . What's that line in the TV commercial? "You never get a second chance to make a first impression."

Candy looked at me as if she thought I was drunk or crazy.

—Only it's worse than that. We don't get any second chances at all. Anyhow, if we did, we'd mess up again. Because your daddy would still be him, and you'd be you, and there'd still be that funny distance stretched out between you. . . .

I was trying to help, to make her see you can't go wishing for nothing, because nothing is all that it gets you. But she burst into sobs like her heart was broke past mending. I made a note to let the barroom philosophy go on by next time—if there ever was a next time, and I got a second chance.

The place Candy directed me to was nearby. It looked like some kind of Moorish castle where they'd shot *The Desert Song,* or one of those old Ronald Colman movies where he's either chasing the A-rabs or they're after him on turbo-camels.

I pulled up at curbside. As Candy dried her eyes and checked her makeup, I just sat a minute and stared up the flight of concrete steps with the ornamental iron rail. At the top were heavily carved double doors stained so dark brown they looked almost black. Above them was an etched rose window with soft red light coming through and falling on the concrete porch below like a puddle of blood.

—So this is where Hollywood proletarians hang out, huh?

—Barrymore used to stay here in the twenties. In the thirties, Marion Davies had the penthouse. Paid for by . . .

—Um, Citizen Kane, right?

—Close, very close. God, when I was growing up, never mind studying the Babylonians . . . that was history.

—From the look of the architecture, maybe some of them Babylonians dropped through, too.

We walked up to the narrow porch. Beside the big carved doors was a set of weathered brass plaques with names on them. I saw Carole Klein's name among others, and one that said:

THE LOYALIST

VIVA LA REPUBLICA!

—Looks like an apartment building, I told Candy.

—It's more like some kind of commune.

—I don't see no bell to ring. Reckon we just walk in?

That's what we did. The door opened and inside there was a wide, tiled foyer and stairs that curved upward out of sight. The walls were dark tan stucco, and framed posters from somebody else's time and place were everywhere. Art Deco men in berets with old-fashioned Mausers and cigarettes hanging off their lips stared out at us like they wanted a password. One guy with wild eyes held up a black flag in one hand and a bayoneted rifle in the other, and above, in old-fashioned lettering, it said POUM.

Off to the left, there was a dimly lighted room with a big fireplace and bookcases everywhere. A fire was burning, and over the mantel, so help me God, was a photograph of Lenin swathed in Soviet flags. The place looked like a workingmen's club I'd visited once in Germany—only with a peculiar political slant.

In the parlor, there were about ten old people sitting on scattered chairs and a sofa near the fire. Some were talking softly, others reading, writing. As we came to the door most of them looked up. The conversation near the fire stopped, and an elderly man got up and slowly walked over to us.

—Can I help you? he asked with a kindly smile.

—Carole Klein, Candy told him almost curtly.

I could see her favorite old family memories didn't include her daddy's agent.

The old man pointed to a woman at a table near the fire. Her back was to the door, but when he called her name, she turned and studied us. He gestured, and Carole Klein rose and came over, no more rapidly than he had.

She had a way of going over you with her eyes that made you wonder if you were the man you reckoned you were. She looked from me to Candy with no sign of greeting. What the hell, when you've been sitting under a picture of Lenin, in

America, as long as she had, maybe you get X-ray eyes. Maybe you come to where you can see through purses and suit coats and spot a federal badge every time. Or maybe she just didn't like anybody very much.

—Miss Klein, I'm Candace Prescott, and this is . . .

Her look stopped Candy. —I don't know any Candace Prescott. You're Candace Hebron, little Miss CIA, she snapped. —What do you want? Is something wrong with Milt?

Candy raised her chin, stared into Klein's eyes.

—My father is dead. They say he committed suicide.

She didn't say it loud, and she sure didn't say it for general consumption, but she hadn't gotten the words out before the other old folks in the room were talking, passing it on, calling it foolishness or a lie, saying they'd seen Milt last week or visited the bookstore only yesterday. A few of them got to their feet, came over, and made a semicircle around us. Carole Klein looked like someone had sprayed her with an old-age potion. All of a sudden, she looked all her seventy years and more.

—Suicide . . . ?

—He left a note. . . . He confessed to having arranged a series of recent murders.

This time the reaction was shocked silence. After it had stretched for what seemed a long time, Carole Klein broke it.

—The newspapers have said nothing about multiple murders.

—The authorities kept them quiet.

—Then it's political. Who died?

—Several prominent conservatives: Will Mohr, Harold Swanson, Louis Werner, Abe Peretz, Nat Wren. And tonight, former Congressman Bearden.

Klein laughed out loud.

—The note's obviously a forgery. A provocation, a stupid piece of counterintelligence.

—Funny you should say that, I put in. —That's just about

the way we see it. Someone wanted Milt Hebron to take the fall. You got any candidates?

Klein gave me one of her patented looks. Maybe when we'd gotten what we had to do done, I'd come back and tell her about offing some of her comrades in the other Berlin. What the hell, with the way things were going back in the U.S.S.R. under Gorbachev, she might think that was just okay.

—How about half the world? Bearden, Mohr, Wren, Peretz . . . God, what a collection of scum.

—Yeah, well, I can see where you're coming from, but we can't put a collar on half the world, sweet thing. We're looking for one man . . . or woman.

She looked at Candy sharply. —Who is this man? CIA also?

—No. Captain Ralph Trapp. New Orleans Homicide. A friend who's helping me investigate my father's death.

That got them all babbling to each other again. I liked it. It made them wonder what was going on. People get to wondering, they say things they don't mean to say.

—Why are you here? Klein demanded. —Surely you don't believe any of us was involved in some kind of revenge plot, do you?

—The folks I usually deal with don't pop people on account of politics, but who knows? Maybe you all are different . . . Check that: I *know* you're different. I just don't know exactly *how* different.

—You can see what we are, Carole said, her tone dripping acid. —We're old, and we're poor. We live on Social Security and whatever comes along. We fight our causes with words, not bullets, Captain Trapp. You'll have to look elsewhere to find out who did this thing—and why.

I had to admit she made a lot of sense, but I wasn't ready to be dismissed yet.

—Candy and I are on our own. The feds are gonna buy the

suicide confession—because they want to close those messy deaths out. The government ain't like the Party. It don't have much of an institutional memory. They'd be happy to blame Hebron and forget the whole thing.

—Why isn't that good enough for you?

—Because . . . a friend of mine got killed. And Milt Hebron didn't do it.

—And I don't want some of the same people who once branded him a traitor now calling him a murderer, Candy put in, her words ringing with passion.

Carole studied us a long moment. Then she took my arm and led me over to a place at the long library table near the fire. Candy followed, and the others found themselves seats where they could listen in.

—All right. We'll help if we can. But first tell me why you suspected us?

—Because whoever killed Milton had to know he had reason to want those men dead. That he'd suffered from those House Un-American Activities hearings.

One of the old men stood up, his face red, his voice shaking. —We all did. Every one of us. The whole country . . .

—When you finish preaching and we all sing the "Internationale" together, I said, —maybe we could get down on it, huh? What I need to find out is who got hurt enough to want to kill the ones that did it, over thirty years later?

—Lots of people. We lost our homes, our jobs, security . . .

—Right, and every time they close down a Chrysler plant, people lose all that. But nobody's gunning for Lee Iacocca and his white-bread vice presidents.

—Pete Small lost his life, an elderly woman said softly. —Pete was a terrific director. They pushed him too far.

The others murmured assent.

—What happened? Candy asked the old woman.

—He had a heart attack during the hearings. He died out in the hallway.

—I was there, the angry old man said, knitting his fingers together. —I wasn't five feet from him. With his last breath he said, "Don't mourn—organize."

—Any survivors?

—No kids. There was a wife. She married Harvey Singer, the producer.

—But aren't they both dead? someone asked.

—I think you're right. I don't remember seeing Harvey's name in the *Hollywood Reporter* for a long time.

—Anyone else? Candy asked.

I was thinking about those names in Hebron's play.

—What about Phil Stern? I asked.

Carole nodded, and the others seemed to agree.

—Phil was at the height of his career. He'd just finished a major film. . . .

—*Under the Double Eagle,* Candy finished softly.

—How did you know? Oh, that's right. It was Milt's screenplay, wasn't it?

Candy nodded. —His last one.

—They tried to make Phil testify against his friends, and he went home and shot himself, one of the old men continued. —With the pistol he'd used at . . . He hesitated, groping in his memory for a name.

Carole Klein looked at him as if she couldn't believe he'd forgotten. —Arganda, Ed, she said in a clipped tone. —The bridge at Arganda. The Fifteenth International Brigade.

And forty years later someone had used that same gun to kill Milt Hebron. I mentally kicked myself for not seeing the connection sooner.

—Who'd Phil Stern leave behind? I asked.

—Nobody, the old man they called Ed said. —No family.

—What about L.K.? Carole asked.

—Who are we talking about? His son?

—His wife. L.K. Stoddard, the director. Don't you know her name?

I looked blank. Candy nodded. —I've heard the name. She was a friend of my father's.

—They both were, Carole came back. —Phil and L.K. were Milt's best friends.

—Where can we find her? I asked.

—Find her? I don't know. She may be dead by now. She left town after Phil killed himself.

—They had something on her, too?

—Of course. They had something on everybody. L.K. had Leftist sympathies. I don't know, maybe she was a Party member. That's what brought her and Phil together.

—L.K. directed *Under the Double Eagle,* didn't she? Ed asked.

Carole shrugged. —That's right. For Warner's. They'd finished the shoot and the post-production just before Phil was subpoenaed. It's in a film can somewhere on the Warner lot—if that collection of Right-wing zombies didn't burn it.

The old man laughed scornfully. —It's there. They never burn anything. What if the country went Left? Then they'd release it . . . a hidden treasure from their proletarian past.

Everything got quiet for a moment. I could hear the crackle of the fire. Then the old man was talking again. In the firelight, the skin of his face was drawn tight along the bones, and maybe from a dozen feet away you'd think he wasn't so old. But he was. His skin had the warm rich quality of old ivory, like some piece from a valuable chess set. I reckoned him for a pawn.

—Blacklisted. All of us. One day, we were the talent in this town. We made the movies. Even the big shots had to pay attention to us. Then the next . . .

He leaned forward and stared at me. —I knew Scott Fitzgerald. We used to have lunch at the commissary. He liked egg salad, and he always had a little flask. And Faulkner. When Bill was writing *The Big Sleep,* he'd come in from Memphis just to . . .

His voice played out then, and the crackle of the fire took over. Maybe he knew it was an old story that everyone had heard, or nobody cared to hear, and Faulkner didn't even live in Memphis. Or maybe he was just tired.

—Doesn't anyone have an idea where we might find L.K. Stoddard? Candy asked almost plaintively. —People don't just vanish.

—They did then, one of the old folks said, voice softer than the rain. —You vanished so you could change your name and get some kind of a job somewhere doing something—till people came to their senses.

—How about a photograph, I asked. —You folks are big on the past. Anybody got a picture of L.K. Stoddard?

They looked at each other and shook their heads. Then Carole Klein brightened, snapped her fingers. —There was a spread when L.K. and Phil were married in Palm Springs. Nineteen-fifty?

The angry old man nodded. —I was there. *Photoplay* covered it, so did *Hollywood Romance.* Warner's PR people saw to it. They were about to begin filming *Under the Double Eagle.*

—Anybody got a copy? I asked.

The laughter was soft, too. Almost sad.

—That's like asking if anybody's got a copy of the *L.A. Times* for June twenty-ninth, 1914, Carole said. —Nobody kept those things.

—Some bookshops have collected them, Candy told me. —Old movie posters, still photos, movie books and magazines . . .

—You want to try Larry Zender's, someone said. —Hollywood Boulevard, east of Vine.

—It'll have to be tomorrow, Carole Klein said. —Nothing's open this late.

As a matter of fact, Art's Deli on Ventura was open. Just another place to park your ass and eat pastrami in L.A., but something else if you're from out of town. We sat in a window booth and watched the counter where they sell bread and cold cuts and chopped chicken liver and the other stuff you wish you had when you're not where it's at.

We'd had a long, bitter day. I asked Candy if she was ready now for me to drop her by her mother's house?

She shook her head no. —I don't want to see her right now.

—What am I missing?

—Maybe it's unfair, but I blame Mother for taking me away from my father all those years ago. Because of her, I grew up in another world from his.

I remembered the manicured lawns and fairy-tale castles in Bel Air. Candy was a princess in the White Zone, for sure. —You'd rather have grown up in back of that bookstore on Fairfax, with old Lefties for friends?

—No. I told you I despised all that foolishness. Daddy let it ruin his career, our family. But even so . . .

Her voice trailed off, but the thought was clear enough. I'd had it myself from time to time. My old man steamed out freight barges on the Mississippi. He walked off on my momma when I was born. He lived not three blocks from the Desire Project, where I grew up. But it might as well have been the dark side of the moon. He never came by, never sent a card or made a call. Not on my birthdays or Christmas, not when I was five or fifteen or any other time.

—Momma, does he know about me?

—He knows, honey. Charlie Trapp knows. Don't put yourself out about it. It's not worth your worry, baby.

—But he's my father. . . .

—No, no, that's not so. That sorry sonofabitch hadn't got a thing to do with you. Your Father is in heaven. . . .

I saw him once. In 1975, down on the Jackson Street Wharf. They called me over to check out a cutting. There was an old man lying with his arms spread out and his eyes staring up into a light rain and his throat cut so deep you could have checked out his neckbones from the front. A cop handed me his empty wallet. Nothing left in it you could spend, but there was a union card for Charles Trapp, who lived on Piety Street.

I'd felt a chill inside like January wind blowing down the river—or like somebody was dancing on my grave. But it didn't matter, and he didn't matter, and I treated it just like I would've if somebody else's old man got done for a few bucks. We never turned up anybody, and we closed the case.

Candy struggled to complete her thought. —I always thought that one day we'd be able to really talk . . . get to know one another.

I shrugged. —Well, that day didn't make it, and if it had, you'd be feeling worse than you do.

The waitress set down our orders, and we got past that moment. I had a cold plate with pastrami and tongue and the salad with a side of chopped chicken liver. Candy had a cheese blintz.

—Deli always puts me in mind of Germany, I said. —There was a butcher shop on Kaiserstrasse. Nothing but sausages. Hundreds of kinds. Names I couldn't pronounce.

—I remember how you loved sausages. I remember the Goldenes Kreuz . . .

Candy put down her fork.

—Rat, can we go to your hotel and go to bed?

I put down my fork. —You wanna finish the blintz and let me get through this tongue?

—No.

Don't ask why I woke up just as the sun was coming at us from somewhere east of Pasadena. Maybe it was ten years in the army. Maybe I was still on New Orleans time. God knows it wasn't because I'd had a dull night.

Our bodies had gotten to know each other twelve years ago in Germany. There was no awkwardness now, no strangeness. Just that good feeling of coming home after a dozen years away. We made love once with urgency, crying out our joy. Then again with tenderness. It seems hours later that exhaustion overwhelmed us. Candy slept, holding on to me tight like a child afraid of getting lost in a crowd.

It was as good as it had ever been for me. I remember falling asleep wondering why I'd turned aside from this sweet lady so long ago.

My dreams reminded me. The woman in my arms had chocolate skin and black hair. And I cried "No" when she whispered, "You know this is the end, Ralph."

I woke up feeling sad, hating to let go of Camille even if she was only a dissolving image in my head.

Candy felt me leaving the bed and reached out to pull me back. —What are you doing?

—My eyes just clicked open, baby. When that happens, I need coffee.

—Room service won't start till seven.

—Dear woman, I got what I need.

In my luggage, I had this little kit I carry everywhere. What you got in there is a small drip pot and a pound of CDM coffee and chicory. I can do without liquor, and if push comes to shove, I can pass on the sex—but CDM is essential.

—Oh my God, I heard Candy call out sleepily from the bed. —Is that the coffee you used to make in Europe?

—Close, but no. That was some off-brand French stuff. This here is the homespun gold.

—I want some.

—There's not enough.

—I'll do something really wonderful for you.

—Maybe I could squeeze out half a cup for you.

—Then you'll get half of what I had in mind.

—You like café au lait?

—O lay? My very favorite kind.

The woman got her coffee, and she didn't lie. I mean she didn't tell a story about what she was gonna do for me.

By the time we finally got dressed, it was going on ten o'clock, and I was anxious to move. Southern boys got hunting in their blood, and I was on a scent.

We were at Larry Zender's shop on Hollywood Boulevard before it opened. A chubby white-haired man was at the door, sorting through his keys as we parked out front. Before I could put a quarter in the meter, Zender'd come up with the key he was looking for and already had his OPEN sign turned around.

—I'm looking for an old *Photoplay* or a *Hollywood Romance*.

—Got a date?

—Nineteen fifty. I'm not sure what month.

Zender shook his head and whistled. —That's got to be a popular period. A college professor was in here just yesterday. You a college professor?

—No. But I've thought about it. When my present employment goes sour, I just might apply.

He walked ahead of us past dusty shelves, into a back room. He turned with a grin and a wave of his hand.

—Magazines, he said. —You got the time to look, you'll probably find what you want. I've been buying old Hollywood for forty years.

—No index file?

—I got to tell you, it's all I can do to keep the books in shape. I mean, this isn't the British Museum Library, is it?

No, I reckoned, it wasn't. It wasn't even the local newsstand for organization.

Candy and I sat down in the dust and started going through magazines that were falling apart even as we picked them up. We found maybe twenty different numbers from the time period Carole Klein and her comrades had suggested. Once, it looked like pay dirt. Candy was sneezing and squinting at a table of contents in a sepia-colored magazine without a cover.

—I think this could be it. . . .

She skimmed through the pages, then dropped the magazine on the floor.

—Goddammit, somebody cut out the pictures.

I picked it up and checked. Sure enough, there was text about the wedding—but somebody had done a number with scissors on the photos. I wondered if that somebody was a fan from long ago—or someone more recent, with a different motive.

—This is no good. Let's spread it out, I told Candy.

She grinned. —Shouldn't we wait till we get back to your place . . . ?

—You ought to be ashamed. This is police work. You're talking off-duty stuff.

We bent to it and got all the magazines sorted out according to date. Zender walked in, looked at the shelves and a big section of floor he probably hadn't seen in twenty years.

—You guys working for me? I mean, look at this. I got to tell you, if you find what you need, it's yours.

We just grinned and kept trucking and turning pages. Then, all of a sudden, I was looking at this handsome dark-haired guy with a warm shy smile. It was a big spread in *Photoplay* on the death of Philip Stern. It told in leering Hollywood-style detail how Stern had been found dead in his bedroom a few hours after his first testimony at the HUAC hearings, a Spanish pistol by his side, a single bullet in his head.

The article quoted all kinds of people—including Nat Wren. Wren had said that HUAC had nothing to do with Stern's death. Phil Stern had been mentally unstable since he'd been captured by Franco's Nationalists in the battle at the Arganda bridge.

It seemed folks played extra rough during the Spanish Civil War, and when the Nationalist intelligence folks found out that Stern was an American Jew, they really unloaded on him. Word was, they had an interrogation adviser sent in from Berlin. You can bet that adviser was Gestapo. He didn't kill Stern, but, according to Wren, he broke him. The next morning a brigade of Nationalists took the Arganda bridge and bayoneted everything in sight—using information Stern had given them.

I guess Stern saw the House Un-American Activities Committee as blood brothers of his Gestapo torturers. He'd escaped them the only way he knew how.

There was a picture of Stern's grave in Forest Lawn. It wasn't clear and it wasn't close, but there was a woman in a loose black dress placing a single red rose in a bud vase. The caption said it was L.K. Stoddard, but it could have just as well been Eleanor Roosevelt or Madonna. Nothing was revealed.

Candy and I looked at one another and shrugged. We'd found the missing lady, and lost her. All on a single page.

The next two hours didn't change anything. All we managed to do was get ourselves covered with the dust of forty years. As we left Larry Zender's shop, it was after noon. He still didn't have many customers. I had to wonder how he could pay the rent. All I could see was a teenager in jeans and a T-shirt that said HOLLYWOOD in one aisle and a woman with a fine ass and a pair of good-looking legs, flipping through some posters at the back of the shop. But Zender seemed happy enough and waved as we left.

I felt frustrated and filthy.

—How about a swim? I asked Candy.

She looked tempted but shook her head no. —I'm going to Mother's, she said. —She wanted to talk about Daddy last night. We've got to do it sometime. I think I'm ready for that now.

—While you're talking about old times, I said, —ask if she knows anything about L.K. Stoddard's whereabouts. If Stern and your daddy were such good friends, maybe she's even got an old photo.

Candy nodded, saying she should've thought of that before wasting half a day sorting through dusty old magazines.

At the Roosevelt, I squirmed into the pair of swimming trunks the hotel supplied—one size fits all, more or less, with a drawstring three feet long. The air was crisp like a New Orleans spring day. The water was colder, but it felt good, and I swam the length of the pool back and forth till the frustration I'd felt turned to fatigue. I heaved myself out of the water and sat a moment catching my breath.

There were eight or ten people around the pool. A couple of round-faced Japanese tourists, the rest middle-aged American moms and pops with kids fresh from the Universal Studio tour, enjoying a relaxing afternoon in the sun before driving down to Disneyland or up to Magic Mountain. A white-coated waiter moved among them, balancing a tray of Cokes and what looked like two brandies. He left the Cokes with the kids, then came over and set the brandies down on the table beside me.

—I didn't order them, I said.

—I did, a voice behind me said.

Jacobs was sitting in a white poolside chair with a big HOLLYWOOD ROOSEVELT towel draped over it. He was wearing a pair of swimming trunks and sunglasses. In the bright sunlight, his fringe of red hair glowed like a halo. I almost laughed out loud. But the really funny thing was, he still looked dangerous.

He gave the waiter a bill and waited till he was out of earshot before speaking.

—The man you killed at the congressman's house became inactive almost a year ago.

—Ruiz? You know that because your people ran him?

—No, but we were kept informed. Call it a matter of . . . theological courtesy.

That pulled a grin out of me. All those little Red bishops just wouldn't feel right if they didn't check in with the big Red pope.

—What does inactive mean?

—Ruiz told his control in Turin he had . . . a personal matter to attend to.

—Since when do revolutionaries take a vacation?

—Excellent point. Dead men on furlough, eh? Questions were raised. Ruiz's answer was that a matter of honor and loyalty had to be taken care of.

I shook my head. Like the techs say, that didn't compute. —Jacobs, are you bullshitting me? 'Cause if you are and I blow your eyes out, all I'm gonna get for it is the Medal of Freedom.

Jacobs gestured and reached out for his brandy. —And a bad conscience. Because sooner or later you'd discover I have told you the truth.

—All right, let's sing a duet on that song for a while. What the hell is this honor and loyalty crap?

That smile of his lit up his face under the red eyebrows and the clipped auburn hair.

—Perhaps you understand that better than I do. After all, you weren't sent into the Democratic Republic to bring out the woman, were you?

He was saying it was a private thing. And he was right. I could understand that better than he could.

—That's all you got?

—Captain, you have too good an opinion of us. We don't control everything any longer. Not since the old days, since the Comintern.

—So you want me to search 'em out and . . .

—Terminate the operation. This is no time for political idiocy.

Jacobs rose, polished off the glass of brandy, and set the glass down turned over on its rim.

—Would you be insulted if I said . . . be careful?

I stood up, too. —No, I told him. —Men in the same trade understand one another. You gonna check in with me if you find out anything more?

He nodded. —Certainly. But if you do my job for me, I'll simply take credit and inform the highest levels of my government that I assisted you with information.

—If they want to check with me, that's the story they'll get.

I shook hands with a KGB man for the second time, and Jacobs walked out of the bright sunlight into a shadowy tunnel that led to the hotel elevators.

Wrapping my towel around my waist, I shoved my feet into my deck shoes. I was figuring on calling Narbonne. Not to report the contact with Jacobs. I was gonna see if I couldn't sweet-talk him into joining the hunt for the missing L.K. Stoddard.

I entered my room through the sliding glass door that opened to the pool area. Across the room, the hall door was propped open by a cleaning cart full of brooms and dusters and bottles and spray cans of all those products you see smiling ladies promoting on TV. From the bathroom came the sounds of a maid scrubbing away at the tiles.

I was sitting on the side of the bed, my back to the bathroom, struggling to get my address book out of my pants pockets, when it suddenly hit me that the bed had already been made up before I went out for a swim. What was a maid doing back in my room at 2 P.M.?

Call me paranoid, but I didn't go ask her. Instead I flipped myself over the bed and landed on my hands and knees on the gray plush carpet on the far side of the mattress from the bathroom. As I did I caught a glimpse of the maid crouched behind the door to the bathroom. Her dark hair slicked back into a net, her crisp white uniform stretched tight over her full breasts and hips. Both arms extended to steady her gun, a silenced .22 automatic pointed in my direction.

I heard only a series of dull thuds as a line of five black holes were punched in the mauve bedspread where I had been sitting a moment before.

She saw she'd missed me and changed her aim. But by then I was flattened out on the floor, digging under the mattress where I'd tucked my Colt Cobra when I went out to swim. I fired without taking the time to pull it clear.

The loud sounds of my shots echoed off the concrete-block walls of my room. I could imagine Japanese and American tourists' heads snapping around at the reports, the waiter grabbing the poolside phone and yelling for hotel security. Fluffy clumps of cotton from the mattress and pieces of ticking and sheet and mauve bedspread exploded out of the bed as the door frame to the bathroom shattered.

Damn. . . . Major Mauvais would have me back on the target practice range in a Shreveport second if he saw that kind of piss-poor shooting. But then I'd never practiced with a mattress over my sight before.

My Wanna-Be Assassin fled the room and was running flat-out down the hall before I could get my Magnum out for a clear shot.

I grabbed a handful of shells from the nightstand and took out after her, but she'd knocked the cleaning cart across the door as she left. I tried to jump over it like O.J. Simpson in those TV commercials, but O.J. has gotta have something I don't. Some damned half-gallon plastic jug of Pine-Sol caught my foot, and I found myself tripping and sliding down the hall on my mostly bare front side. I could feel the rough carpet fibers scraping away the skin on my chest and thighs. Shit. If I'd known I was gonna be body surfing on nylon, I'd have slapped on some greasy suntan lotion when I was at the pool.

By the time I regained my feet, the Wanna-Be had disappeared through a door on the far side of the hall.

It led to the parking lot back of the hotel. Outside, a big blue dumpster almost blocked the door. Beyond it were rows and rows of shiny-clean new cars. They started at the hotel canopy and stretched all the way to the street behind the hotel. Nothing moved except for red-jacketed Latino kids scurrying around to fetch Mercedeses and Jaguars for hotel guests. Somewhere, behind or in one of those cars, that good-looking woman who'd tried to kill me was hiding.

I was checking the row of cars nearest me when, from out on Orange Street, I heard the sound of a door slamming and a car peeling away from the curb. It was a black Chrysler New Yorker. And if it wasn't the same car that belonged to the sniper at the beach, it was a kissing cousin.

I ran across the asphalt to the cashier's window. A plump middle-aged Latino lady looked at me with wide, alarmed eyes. I pointed to my key chain hanging on a board with others. She handed it over without argument. I guess an almost-nude black man waving a gun seemed reason enough not to demand a parking ticket or payment.

A couple of nicely dressed guests waiting to pick up their expensive transportation watched slack-jawed as I vaulted into my rented Mercedes convertible and drove off. I figured my jaunt through the Roosevelt lot just became a prominent part of Hollywood lore that'd be told and retold all winter at Garden Club and Rotary meetings back in Kansas City or Cincinnati.

At Sunset Boulevard, the light was green, but there was no sign of the black Chrysler. That was okay. I'd recognized that ass and those legs from Zender's shop. And though I hadn't gotten a good look, I was pretty sure I could put a face with the body. I turned west toward the Pacific coast. I had a good idea where to find my Wanna-Be lady killer. And I was betting that L.K. Stoddard would be close by.

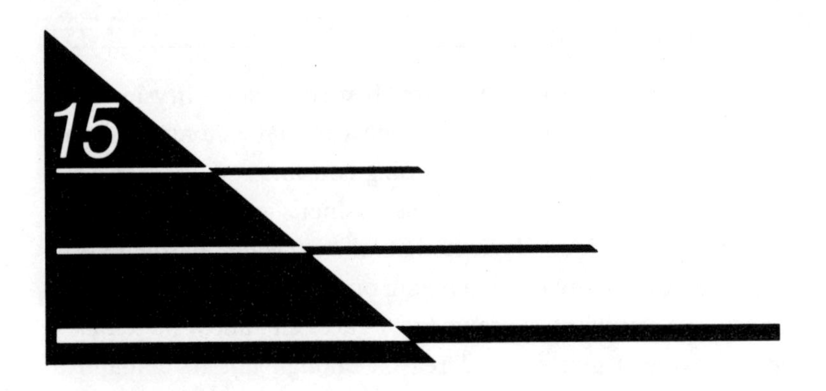

I got to admit my blood was up. Like on my first hunt when I was a twelve-year-old kid. Some of my momma's people still sharecropped in the Delta in those days. That was before the Movement improved things for such black folks. As I recall, my aunt and her family later moved into New Orleans and took to living on welfare in the St. Thomas Project. But back in the fifties they lived in a falling-down wooden shack in Mississippi, near Picayune, and worked in the fields sunup to sundown. Their usual sport was fishing for bream or catfish or shooting squirrel on weekends. Only with a city visitor to entertain, they planned something special.

They took me out in the woods in an old pre–World War Two Ford pickup and let the hounds loose. And soon the dogs went to baying and running, and we followed, bouncing and crashing through the woods after them in that pickup. I was in back and holding on for dear life as tree branches grabbed my clothes and tried to pull me out.

Then the dogs cornered some small critter. They were snarling and fighting and tearing it to pieces before we reached them. My uncle took a baseball bat to the dogs, then held up a bloody pelt for me to admire. As he smeared my face with the warm blood, I grinned ear to ear. I always get that same good feeling when a manhunt is nearing its climax.

Sunset Boulevard was usually a chore to drive. Today the midafternoon traffic was light, and I had no trouble getting past the closed comedy clubs and bars and restaurants along The Strip. They looked seedy and dead now, but would resurrect like some horror-movie vampire once the sun drowned itself in the Pacific.

I hit the big, wide esplanaded part of Sunset that winds through Beverly Hills, and floored the Mercedes. The mansions lining the street were the size of government buildings. I wondered if the sweet smell in the air came from the magnolias that were still in bloom or if it was the smell of money.

The road got narrow and twisted as it went through Bel Air, but I didn't slow any—till I heard the sound of a siren behind me. My speedometer was on 55. Okay for the freeway, but bad news if a city patrol wanted to fuck with me.

It occurred to me about then that I'd left my wallet and badge back in the hotel room when I took out after that hit woman with the great ass. I remembered how Henry Harleaux had said that respectable black people weren't really welcome in the White Zone. So I couldn't help but wonder how the L.A.P.D. would greet a seminude black man with no I.D. and a .357 Magnum Colt Cobra?

I didn't get a chance to find out. Instead of a black and white, the siren belonged to an ambulance. As I slowed, it pulled around me and kept on going down Sunset like it was being called to the Last Judgment. The paramedic on the passenger side did give me a curious second look as they passed. He'd probably use his mike to call in a suspicious-character report. But it didn't matter 'cause I didn't plan to stay around long enough for a patrol car to find me.

Only my plans got changed when I saw the ambulance turn onto Bellagio Drive. Whoever had followed me to Zender's store had seen Candy with me. And if I was enough of a threat for them to try a daytime wet operation, she just might be a target, too. So I hit the brakes and spun my wheel, and my Mercedes fishtailed into the turn right after the ambulance. Sure enough, it turned into a side street and pulled to a stop before Seventeen Bellagio Terrace.

I think the sight of me following them froze those white paramedics in the ambulance a minute. All I know is I reached those big carved double doors long before they did.

They were unlocked. As I went into the foyer I heard Candy's voice calling out from somewhere up that curving staircase that led to the second floor. She sounded scared or in pain.

—Up here. . . . Hurry, please. . . .

I took the stairs two at a time, noticing as I did that the portraits of Candy that lined the wall got younger and younger. It was like a journey back through time. The last showed her as a chubby baby in a white lace-trimmed dress. The familiar gunmetal hair was hidden under a cap. Only something about the dark eyes staring boldly at the camera told me it was Candy.

There she was at the head of the stairs. Her hair damp, dressed in an orange cotton jumpsuit like some fashion designer's idea of what a well-dressed parachutist might wear. And, thank the Lord, she looked unhurt.

—Rat, what are you . . . ?

—Somebody just took a couple of shots at me. I got worried about you.

—I'm all right. It's . . . I called an ambulance . . .

—Paramedics right behind me.

And they were. Still looking apprehensive, two guys in uniform were creeping up the stairs carrying a folded-up gurney.

—In the bedroom, Candy directed them. —Hurry . . .

We entered together this massive room that could have passed for a *Dynasty* set. The walls and drapes and upholstery and bed hangings and bed cover were all done in a matching blue-and-white print fabric. A crystal chandelier bigger than you see in most ballrooms hung over the king-size bed. To one side, a dressing alcove was tiled in white marble veined with gold, and the gold-plated fixtures looked like they'd come from Tiffany's. And all this luxury was doubled in the mirrors that covered the alcove's walls and ceiling.

I saw Elaine Prescott's reflection before I saw her. She lay stretched out across the quilted blue-and-white bed cover. A pool robe and a still-damp swim suit were crumpled on the white plush carpet beside the bed. She was nude, a light bikini line across her hips contrasting with her tanned legs and back. Her body was softly plump, but for a woman who was almost sixty, she had little to be ashamed of.

—I don't know what happened, Candy sobbed. —She was at the pool when I came home. I told her I was going to shower and then we'd talk. . . . Oh, God, did she have a stroke or a heart attack?

One of the paramedics felt for a pulse. —Thready pulse, shallow breathing. Looks like an O.D. to me.

He picked up a prescription container from the table that stood at bedside. —Halcion. The prescription was for thirty capsules, but there're none left. Does she have a history of attempting suicide?

—No, no . . . Mother never did anything like that. That can't be what it is.

—We'll take her to the nearest E.R. They can tell from a blood test what she took.

As the paramedics started an I.V. and covered Elaine Prescott with a blanket, I put my arms around Candy.

—Was anyone else in the house?

—I don't know. I guess Mother's maid was, but I didn't see anyone.

—Did you ask her about L.K. Stoddard?

Candy looked at me with a confused wide-eyed expression that reminded me of that baby girl on the wall at the head of the stairs.

—I was going to as soon as I . . . Oh, no, it's not like what happened to Daddy, is it?

I pulled Candy to me and held her tight as the paramedics carried a pale, unconscious Elaine Prescott from her blue-and-white bedroom.

—You go on with your momma to the hospital. You're gonna want to be there when she comes to and tells you what went down.

—Rat, what if she doesn't . . . come to?

—Then tell the doctors to do a real careful autopsy. Look for an injection point. I'm betting this suicide attempt is as fake as your daddy's.

I got Candy downstairs and into that ambulance with Elaine Prescott, glad she was too upset to ask where I was headed next. I knew I didn't have enough for a warrant, and I didn't need Candy, Narbonne, and the ABC agencies telling me so. I was looking for justice, not law.

It was good the house on Mountain Way was so secluded. Nosey neighbors wouldn't be butting in. I drove past the place real slow, sizing up the high cinder-block wall that ringed the estate. I was looking for a place where the pines and eucalyptus overhanging it might give me a little help in scaling the wall—but they'd all been carefully trimmed back.

About then I regretted being a smart-ass and renting a convertible. Starting from the hardtop of my Olds, I could have easily made it over that seven-foot wall.

When the cinder blocks ended, I turned the Mercedes around in the next drive where a big sliding electric gate kept out unwanted visitors like me. Those folks had them a fancy wrought-iron fence. Wrought iron cost more than cinder blocks, and the neighbor's fence was only about five feet high. I parked and climbed on the hood of my car, leaving a little dent for the rental agency to cluck over, and vaulted over the metal spikes. I landed and rolled on soft grass that looked like a well-kept putting green.

On this side of that cinder-block wall, nobody had bothered trimming the trees. Shinnying up a pine was a damned sight easier when I was a kid, but I congratulated myself on still having enough stuff left, thirty years later, to do it without breaking into a sweat.

I dropped quietly into the di Silva estate not too far from the big six-car garage. A limo and a couple of smaller cars half filled it, but so far as I could see, ole Handlebar Mustache, the chauffeur, wasn't around. Good. I didn't need a firefight announcing me.

I considered checking out the garage for some spare work clothes. I can't say I ever carried out a guerrilla raid in swim trunks before. A nice coverall would have suited me better.

But my vanity about clothes almost did me in. I was five steps toward the garage when the front door to the house opened and Handlebar Mustache comes out carrying two boxes in his arms, an Uzi slung over his shoulder. I had to dive back behind some thick azalea bushes for cover. A woman's voice talking rapid Italian followed the guy out the open door. From her tone she was telling him to hurry. He opened the trunk of the limo and stowed the boxes, then returned double-time to the house.

Since he'd left the trunk open, he was clearly coming back with more boxes or bags. This was too busy a spot to linger.

Moving from bush to bush, tree to tree, I circled around the side of the house, looking for another way in.

It was a big half-timbered house that looked like it belonged on a hilltop in Switzerland, not in the middle of a grove of eucalyptus in Bel Air. If I had any sort of equipment, I could have scaled up the exposed beams to some unlocked window and worked from the top down. It's not like me to be unprepared, but you gotta remember I come to California for a vacation. Maybe I should've stopped at some hardware store on Sunset Boulevard and bought me a set of house-breaking tools. Hell, come to think of it, I didn't have any cash or credit cards with me, either.

All the time I'm scouting the house I'm also looking out for guards. That Uzi the chauffeur was carrying didn't promise lax security. But I didn't see a one. Packing for a run beyond Uncle Sam's reach had to be distracting them. Or maybe there was electronic surveillance I couldn't spot.

Well, crouching there in the bushes undecided till they loaded up the limo and drove away wasn't gonna cut it. I had to make a move. I spotted a two-story brick chimney with wisteria growing all the way up it. The mat of interlocking vines looked like the rope net my D.I. had us climb in Basic when I was nineteen. Next to the chimney, on the second story, was a balcony. I'd done that seven-foot wall. Who says I couldn't do a thirty-foot chimney as readily and ease onto that balcony?

Halfway up, with vines snapping under my hands and old brick crumbling away under my feet, I got to wishing real hard I was nineteen again. Even in the dry California air, this time I was sweating when I reached the top.

With a small prayer of thanks to St. Jude, patron of hopeless causes, I swung over the wooden railing and collapsed onto the balcony. The only cover was a rattan sofa with fat canvas cushions. It wouldn't stop even a .22 slug, but it might shield me from casual view.

Open French doors led from the balcony into a room. From inside I could hear recorded voices with music in the background. A sound track? Who would be taking time to watch TV when they were in the process of clearing out?

It was Signora di Silva, that's who. Only I was sure now that, before she married her Italian movie producer, she was a.k.a. L.K. Stoddard.

And it wasn't TV she was watching. It was a movie. And an old one, by the shaky looks of it.

The room was a bedroom, nicely done by some decorator in brocades and French antiques twenty years ago, but a little old and faded now. The house looked like it had been rented-out furnished for a long time. In the middle of the floor somebody had set up a movie projector on a metal cart. L.K.'s back was to me, and past her turbaned head I could see black-and-white figures moving across a portable screen.

The actors were all in period clothes, dressed real shabby like poor workers before the turn of the century. A face I recognized from that *Photoplay* magazine spread suddenly filled the screen. Philip Stern was talking to a group of miners huddled around a fire. A hard, cold Rocky Mountain wind was blowing, trying to whip his words away. Words I knew Milt Hebron had to have written.

Down in Memphis they hustled me off a freight and found my red card, and they tried to burn me alive. But I found me a brother there, and we come out of it all right. And you'll see, it'll be all right here, too. Because we're the future. Because we're the end of them all. Because, in the night while they try to sleep, we're walking up and down singing out the Brotherhood. They doze and dream and hear our voices increased a thousandfold. They hear the groans of yesterday, the shouts of today, the exultation of tomorrow. And they wake with sweat as cold as snow coursing down their backs and freezing under the arms. What will we do with them? they wonder. What will we do tomorrow when the day dawns red?

Then that five-foot-two Italian bombshell with the great ass stomped into the room and stood in front of the screen, scowling at L.K. She was still in the white maid's uniform she had on when she took those five shots at me. The light from the projector played over her body, and Phil Stern's face was distorted by the swells of her breasts.

She said something in rapid Italian. Hers was the same voice I'd heard scolding the chauffeur. L.K. replied in English without the accent she'd put on for Candy and me.

—I have nothing to pack. Everything I value is right here.

L.K. touched the projector at her side. The younger woman spun on her heel and left as fast as she'd come. I figured it was time to interrupt the feature for a commercial.

I stepped into the bedroom and pulled the projector's plug out of the wall socket. As the screen went dark, L.K. turned her ancient head toward me, looking for all the world like one of them 200-year-old tortoises the *National Geographic* likes to photograph.

She showed no surprise at the sight of me, even me in my white bathing trunks.

—When Anna Maria told me she'd missed you, I feared you might have recognized her.

—The face almost escaped me, but I never forget a good-looking ass.

—You don't look like a man who would. I didn't want to use her, but Pino insisted. I think he feared leaving her alone in Italy.

—Probably with good reason. Pino's the chauffeur?

—No, that's Joachim. Pino is my technician.

—He's the one who took that film of Camille's death?

—Ah, Camille Bynum. The woman you cared for. Her death was a mistake.

—I know, but somebody's gonna pay, anyway.

—So you seek revenge? Good. You'll understand when I say, I do, too.

—That's why you were there at the dedication in person? You wanted to *see* Wren die.

—Wren more than Bearden, Mohr, or any of the others.

—Because of the HUAC hearings?

—Because they deserved to die. Mohr denounced Phil to Bearden's committee. Then Bearden and his flunkies, Swanson and Wren, they tore Phil apart.

—I hear your husband killed himself.

—Because he knew what was coming. SAG was already demanding Phil sign a loyalty oath. Peretz was threatening to fire us, blacklist us, if Phil refused to betray his comrades.

She gestured weakly toward the projector with her bony arm. —Warner refused to release our last film. That's the only remaining print of *Under the Double Eagle.* Hardly a day has passed I haven't looked at it. To remember, to plan my revenge.

There's an old Sicilian saying. Revenge is a dish best served cold. This woman had kept hers in a deep freeze almost forty years.

—You sure took your time about it.

—I couldn't do it by myself. They were all powerful men. I needed money. Until Carlo died, I had none of my own.

—So your terrorist friends came along for the money?

—They owed me for past favors. Besides, killing a capitalist pig or robbing a bank are means to the same end.

—And killing unsuspecting old men is easier than going up against armed guards, right?

I finally said something that riled her. Her dark eyes shone with hatred.

—Those *old men* destroyed me—my career, the man I loved.

—Milt Hebron didn't. I hear he was a friend, a fellow sufferer.

—You showed him that film. Milt recognized me. He called and asked to talk. To *talk* . . . as if words could stop me. As if anything could stop me except . . .

She laughed a short, bitter coughing sound, then lifted an ashy hand to push back her turban a little to show a hairless skull. —I'm dying. But I'll see all my enemies precede me to hell.

—Forget it. It's done with, I said as I reached for the phone and dialed 911.

—No, not yet, L.K. answered. The wrinkles on her turtle face rearranged themselves into something like a smile. Then I realized the line had gone dead.

—Pino doesn't trust me completely. He monitors the phone.

Coming down the hall, I heard the sound of running feet.

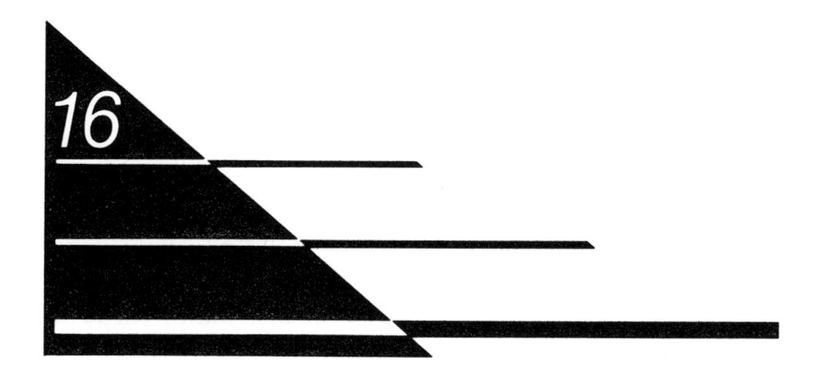

16

L.K. called out something in Italian.

The running steps abruptly stopped.

—I should kill you for that, I said, pulling my .357 out of the waistband of my swim trunks.

L.K. threw me a look somewhere between amusement and contempt. —I'd welcome death.

—Then I won't make it so easy on you. I turned my attention to the hall.

They taught me in the army that a good offense is better than getting shot sitting on your ass. I jerked open the hall door and gave a good hard push to the stand holding the movie projector. It rolled into the hall, where a burst of automatic weapon fire hit and toppled it, ten or twelve shots smashing it to rubble.

Behind me, I heard a wail of anguish from L.K. as she saw her beloved reel of film being demolished. I sensed more than saw her getting unsteadily to her feet, flinging herself forward as if to protect the film with her own frail body. I sure didn't need her cluttering up the fire zone. I backhanded her as she tried to pass me. She was light as a feather and went flying like

Peter Pan back into the room. I didn't wait to see if she hit her chair or the floor before I launched myself into the hall.

Something big and ugly was looming midway down the hall, and I fired my Colt Cobra three times in that general direction before I come up hard against the opposite wall.

There was a low bookcase full of a nice set of matching leather tomes that looked like they'd never been opened. I wedged my six-foot frame behind it as best I could and peeked over the top. A marble bust of some old Roman or Greek with curly hair and a fine straight nose gave me enough cover for a peek at who was shooting at me.

L.K. had said his name was Pino, but I recognized him as that big sonofabitch from the Athena bar, old Smoking Jacket. And I had thought he was just an ugly queer sweet on me. How wrong can you be? He must have heard me asking for Wren. He'd been running interference while one of his comrades out in the parking lot drained Nat Wren's crankcase.

My shots had knocked Pino down but not out. His legs were crumpled under him, and the beige carpet was being stained red by a spreading pool of his blood. But, as I watched, his ugly face twisted in a grimace and his huge muscular torso reared up like a cobra and filled half the hall. Then his Uzi came up off the floor and chattered again.

The marble bust where my head had been a second before burst and rained sharp stone fragments down on my head and bare shoulders. They stung, but not nearly so much as one of them Uzi 9mm slugs would have.

Now I don't go swimming with a bandolier of .357 Magnum bullets strung around my chest like Rambo, so I was running real low on ammo. I had grabbed a handful of shells as I left my hotel room and shoved them in the pocket of my swim trunks, but I'd used all but one to reload with on the way here. The Colt Cobra was already half empty. If I didn't watch out, my worst nightmare was gonna come true—I'd be facing an enemy with no bullets in my gun. I had to quit fooling around popping off shots and kill that sucker.

With both hands on my Magnum, arms straight out to steady it like they teach the greenhorns at the academy, I jumped to my feet, whirled, and aimed at the chest of that motherfucker with the Uzi.

He was as big as a barn and twenty yards away. How could I miss? I didn't, and my two shots bumped him backward as they hit—but he still didn't fall over on his back and play dead. Shit. He was big, but nobody's big enough to stand up to two .357 Magnum slugs in the chest. Was he wearing body armor? If so, I had to make a head shot before he got that Uzi firehose going in my direction again or I was a dead man.

I saw that Uzi coming up and filled my sight with the ugliest face I'd seen since last time I visited the baboons in Audubon Zoo. My arms jerked as I fired the last .357 Magnum slug in my Colt. His head snapped and a gout of blood and gray tissue hit the wall behind him and slid slowly down and plopped onto that beige carpeting.

Pino wouldn't be needing that Uzi anymore, but I would. I tucked my Colt Cobra back in the waistband of my swim trunks and checked the clip of the semiautomatic. It still had about twenty shots left.

The sound of the shooting had been plenty loud. I could hear excited shouts in Italian, and the sound of running feet on the first floor. They were headed toward the wide stairway I could see back of Pino. I knew the maid and the chauffeur were still left to deal with. I dearly hoped the high price of domestic help had limited the staff to just those two.

I turned and headed away from those front stairs. I didn't know about Bel Air mansions, but the old uptown New Orleans houses always had rear stairs for the servants. I remembered, as a boy, carrying freshly starched and ironed shirts up the rear stairs at Narbonne's house when my momma used to work for his.

Sure enough, around a turn in the hall was a narrow twisting stairway that led down to a sort of pantry next to the kitchen.

The kitchen was immense, like an army mess instead of a private home. Two gleaming stainless steel refrigerators, two old-fashioned-looking, black iron gas ranges. And a white tile work island in the middle of the room with a big metal rack hanging down from the ceiling above, full of giant copper and stainless steel pots and pans. Before the owners started renting out the place, this house must have seen some damned fancy dinner parties. Hadn't L.K. told Candy and me that Douglas Fairbanks, Sr., had once lived there?

Jesus, what a dumb-assed thought, what with two terrorists on my tail. Breathing the L.A. smog must do that to your brain. Next thing you know, I'd be out buying one of those maps to the homes of the stars they sell on street corners. Hell, I might be lucky if I was able to do that.

There was a door from the kitchen to the outside that sorely tempted me. I opened it quietly, then let it slam closed. From the front part of the house, I heard those scurrying feet again. Either this place had really big rats, or somebody was headed my way.

Sure enough, Handlebar Mustache, Uzi off his shoulder and at the ready, rushed into the kitchen. He gave a quick glance around, then kept on going out the back door, looking around the yard for me. But I'd retreated a little ways out of sight up that narrow stairway, and now his back was to me. I know what I should've done, but I'm sorry. I grew up on Tom Mix and Gene Autry Saturday movie serials. The Code of the West says you don't shoot a man in the back. I just had to call out to him.

—Hey, motherfucker . . .

He turned, looking surprised to see me still standing in the doorway. Worried about that possible body armor, I sort of sprayed the Uzi up and down. It wasn't a real accurate gun, but it made up for poor quality with generous quantity. The snail drum held fifty 9mm Parabellum bullets when it was full. I'd shot twenty rounds and he'd taken at least ten hits before he crumpled to the ground and my clip come up empty. I hung the empty Uzi from a hook on that big metal rack with all the shiny pots and pans and went outside after Handlebar's gun.

But as I bent to pick it up, a shot hit the gun and knocked it away from my hand. I hadn't heard a report, so I figured it was that silenced .22 speaking out again in its quietly authoritative way. I knew from the hotel that the shooter wasn't that great a shot. The bullet must have been meant for me and hit the gun by accident. Another slug ricocheted off the paving at my feet, and a third one hissed by my ear like an angry cottonmouth water moccasin. Give that woman enough time, she might actually home in on her target and ream me a new one.

I forgot the Uzi and dived behind a raised flower bed where masses of white, yellow, and bronze chrysanthemums were budding and just beginning to burst into bloom.

A fourth and fifth silenced shot chipped at the native stones that had been mortared together to make a retaining wall for the flower bed. It was barely a foot high but offered the only cover within ten yards. Through the green foliage of the mums, I could see the shooter was at an open ground-floor window near the front of the house, but keeping well back of the frame and out of sight. A sixth .22 shot grazed my rear with a searing pain and made me jump, then hunker down even lower to the ground. Damn, my swimming trunks had been sticking up above the rock wall like a white flag of surrender. It wasn't but a flesh wound, but it showed that little Italian lady could hit a bull in the ass if he gave her a still target.

Hugging the ground as best I could, I fished out the one .357 Magnum cartridge left in the pocket in my swimming trunks. It was an armor-piercing round. My hand was red with my own blood as I loaded the shell into my Colt Cobra. I watched the curtain at the window move as a seventh shot was fired. The shooter had to be about a foot to the left of that window. I remembered she was only five-foot-two, lowered my sights, and fired.

There was a faint cry. Was that a little playacting on her part to lure me out from my cover? I scrambled to my feet, but stayed hunched over like a sprinter, ready to drop if that .22 spoke again. But there was only silence. The .357 Magnum AP round had gone right through the wall and hit home.

As I sprinted across the yard my feet squished in my deck shoes. Blood was oozing from my flesh wound, running in a dark red rivulet down my leg and into my shoe. I reached again for Handlebar's Uzi, meaning to go check out the rest of the house, but there was this big crashing sound from the direction of the front gate. Two black-and-whites, running silent with their red lights whirling, sped up the drive and skidded to a halt just like they do in *Police Academy*. Fuck it. Let the local boys see if there was a cook with a .45 or a gardener with a bazooka. This wasn't my beat, anyway.

No, this was the White Zone that those voices at the airport had warned me about. Those boys in blue tumbled out of their cars and lined up behind their hoods with their weapons drawn and pointed—at *me.*

—Police . . . You're covered . . . Throw down your gun. . . .

The voice doing the yelling was high-pitched like a teenager's. Not wanting to alarm these nervous whiteboys any more than necessary, I put up my hands—my Colt Cobra in my left hand, that Uzi in my right. Then I tossed them real soft and easy toward the speaker.

—Keep cool, men, I'm not armed.

—Watch him, he might have a hideout gun.

Yeah, sure, like up my ass. I just stood there, dripping blood, waiting for one of them brave patrolmen to step up and ask me to drop my drawers. One of the four was a cute female cop. I hoped she'd be the one who pulled that job.

No such luck. A towheaded fresh-faced kid who looked like he belonged on a marine recruiting poster inched forward and kicked my Magnum and the Uzi out of reach.

—Down on your face, he ordered.

—Look, there's no need of that, I tried to explain.

Only he didn't want to hear any explanation. His nightstick caught me upside my head, and I dropped to my knees. Then another blow across the back of my head buried my face in the dirt. Harleaux had been right about the L.A.P.D. They look clean-scrubbed, but they play real dirty.

The marine handcuffed me as the other three spread out and checked the house.

—One dead male by the back door, someone yelled.

—There's a woman fatally wounded in the library. I'm going upstairs now, the female cop sang out from inside the house.

—You're one mean motherfucker, aren't you? my cop hissed as he twisted the cuffs and aimed a kick at my groin.

I wanted to tear his dick off and shove it down his throat till he choked to death, but that pleasure would have to wait till I could get some officer to listen to me and check my story with Narbonne.

Then the female cop came out helping L.K. down the steps like she was her long-lost grandmother.

—There's another dead male in the upstairs hall. This poor old woman seems to be the only survivor—and I'm afraid she's about to have a heart attack.

L.K. did look like she was five minutes from hell. I guess her turban had come off when I shoved her down. Her almost hairless bony skull looked like what they paint on packages of rat poisoning to scare off children. And she was clutching the front of her dress like she was in pain. But her stagey recoil when she saw me and the phony Italian accent she put on convinced me it was all an act.

—The black man . . . He broke into my bedroom. . . . A rapist . . . My servants . . . Pino and Joachim and Anna Maria . . . they try to protect me. He kill them. . . . If you no come, he kill me. . . .

She began to tremble and weep and pull at her chest. It was no Academy Award performance, but it was good enough to sucker that female cop.

—It'll be all right. I'll call for an ambulance and . . .

—Help me. . . . I can no breathe, L.K. gasped and rolled her eyes and sagged against the female cop. She would have hit the ground if another cop hadn't jumped to catch her.

—Get her in the car, Joe. I'll start CPR, and you get us to the nearest E.R. . . . ASAP.

—Don't fall for that grandmother act, I said. —She's faking. The Secret Service want her for seven or eight killings. And those weren't her servants. They were hired terrorists.

I might as well have saved my breath. My words sounded fucking incredible even to me. Four pairs of blue eyes glared at me.

—You crazy black bastard, was all I heard. Then that nightstick cracked into my skull again. I figured the marine had to play tennis. He had one hell of an overhead smash.

Of course the sonsofbitches apologized. Much later, at the station. After Harleaux recognized me and chewed some ass, and Narbonne showed up and threw some of that federal bull around. The marine with the quick nightstick was especially repentant. He was sweating blood and crapping in his pants as he saw his future as police chief vanishing before his eyes. They'd been responding to a neighbor's report of shots fired, he explained. Why shouldn't they think the one left standing with an Uzi and a .357 Magnum had been the one who started it all?

That made sense, and I might have gone easier on him if it'd just been me involved. I've been known to nail a few perps myself when they gave me incredible lip. But the sad fact was, they'd let L.K. give them the slip.

While I was slaphappy, Miss Bleeding Heart had carried the old woman into the U.C.L.A. emergency room. Only L.K. had walked out on her own as soon as the cop turned her back.

So I played D.I. to the marine. I chewed him to the bone and spit out the pieces. I told him being a lawman is a business, not a sport. I cracked his nuts for assaulting a suspect, for aiding the escape of a felon, for being a honkie racist, and for just generally being dog-shit dumb.

When all I had left to say was his daddy didn't love him and his momma dressed him funny, I realized I'd run out of insults and anger at about the same time. I sent the kid packing and filled in Narbonne on what had happened.

—You I.D. those dead fuckers?

—The two men were Pino di Napoli and Joachim Barzilla. Both had long records with Interpol. *Brigata Rossa.* The woman, no. She was a novice, a hanger-on.

Like I'd thought, a Wanna-Be terrorist. I don't like killing a woman, especially one five-foot-two with a fine ass. If I'd had a clean shot at her, I could have decommissioned her without killing her. Well, like I'd told Candy, you don't get to do things twice.

—At least this clears Candy's old man, right?

—Well . . . , Narbonne said, putting on his bureaucratic face.

—Hebron should have told us he recognized L.K. Stoddard in that film. That has to show a certain sympathy for her cause.

—He died for his bad judgment. Ain't that enough?

—I'll do what I can to get the Agency to dump all the blame on the Stoddard woman. You'll have to give me a full report on everything she said and . . .

—Fuck that, Alphonse. She'll tell you everything herself. She's proud of what she's done. Just find her. Think you can do that?

That bureaucratic shrug again. —No way she can leave the country. I alerted the Border Patrol and Immigration.

—That wasn't what I asked.

—Hell, it's a big city, a bigger country.

—If the Secret Service can't cut it, maybe you should get *America's Most Wanted* to flash her picture on TV.

That chapped him a little, but he tried not to let it show. —Sooner or later we'll get a lead. I'm not worried.

—Then you're stupid. L.K. killed seven people. Or is it eight?

—No, Candy's mother made it. She's in Cedars Sinai. But you pulled Stoddard's fangs. She's just a solitary old woman now. There're no *Brigata Rossa* terrorists for hire in L.A.

—Then tell me why I feel so uncomfortable.

—You're just pissed you didn't wrap this up single-handed. But trust me. It's over. *Fini.* Unless you want a medal or something.

Shit. All I wanted was to get back on a Delta plane and fly home and celebrate my safe return from the White Zone with a strip sirloin and a plate of French-fried onions at Charlie's. But first I had a couple of good-byes to say.

Candy wasn't at home when I called the next morning, so I looked for her in her mother's hospital room. Or I guess I should say suite.

Elaine Prescott was at Cedars Sinai, a big modern twin-tower hospital on the border of Beverly Hills and West Hollywood. They had to be used to catering to celebrities. The Prescott suite had a separate sitting room with a nice sofa, a basket of fruit on the table, an extension phone, and even a little refrigerator to keep the wine and cheese cool. I bet the bathroom had avocado soap and honeydew melon shampoo. It was so nice it almost made me want to check in for some of that rest I'd come to L.A. for. I could get cosmetic surgery on that nick in my butt.

Mrs. Prescott was wearing a little more than when I'd last seen her. A tailored blue-silk dressing gown that probably cost as much as my suit. But she was still pale beneath her tan, and her grip as she took my hand was weak. It seemed Candy had gone to her father's temple. His friends were saying Kaddish for him.

—Those horrible people almost killed me, too, Elaine Prescott said, a shiver of recalled horror shaking her.

—You saw who did it?

—He grabbed me from behind, but I caught a glimpse of him in the dressing room mirror as he jabbed a hypodermic in my thigh. He was huge . . . and very ugly.

—I know just who you mean. His name was Pino something or other. You don't have to worry about him anymore. He's dead.

She looked relieved, then miffed. —Candace must have known that, but she didn't say a word. She's that way about her work. Very secretive.

—Maybe she takes the Agency a bit too seriously.

—I think she does. I always felt by picking that kind of career she was trying to prove something—to Milt, maybe to herself. Anyway, will you tell me, Captain Trapp? Why did they do it?

I never held with all that government secret stuff. Mostly it's to cover up bureaucratic stupidities.

—Got anything to drink in that refrigerator?

—Please help yourself. Some friends brought me a nice Chardonnay.

It was no Black Bush, but it was cool and crisp. I filled me a water glass full and gingerly eased myself down on that sofa, and proceeded to tell the lady everything I knew about L.K. Stoddard and her jolly band of Italian terrorists.

—As to why they come after you, I can only guess. Maybe L.K. was afraid Hebron said something to you about her. Or maybe Pino just mistook you for Candy.

—I can't believe L.K. would have . . . , Elaine started, then fell silent. She fetched a second water glass, and poured herself a good slug of that Chardonnay.

—Captain Trapp, I want to tell you something. And I want your advice on whether or not I should tell Candace.

Then she laid some incredible rap on me.

It seems L.K. Stoddard had been pregnant when Phil Stern committed suicide. I remembered that photo of her putting a rose on his grave in Forest Lawn. So that's why she was wearing that loose black dress. When the baby was born, L.K. had left her infant daughter with Elaine and Milt Hebron when she decamped to Europe. They'd named her Candace, and never told her she was adopted.

I had to wonder what kind of woman L.K. was to abandon the baby of the man she loved above all others. I guess the answer had to be the kind who'd kill seven people in the name of love.

In the service, I'd seen a thousand old European monuments honoring martyrs who had been killed for the love of Christ by other Christians. I had a hunch L.K.'s love for Phil Stern was of that same sick, twisted kind. She hadn't loved a mere man, she'd loved a proletarian hero, a celluloid crusader. She'd turned the events around his suicide into some kind of passion play where Phil died for undeserving mankind. She'd worshipped at his altar daily by playing that old film of his over and over. And I suspected, if the truth were known, the killings weren't so much to avenge the wrong done him, as to make a prominent role for herself in the drama.

—So what do you think, Captain Trapp?

I thought Hollywood and all the crazy people in it who believed the myths they made up were full of shit. But that wasn't what Elaine Prescott was asking.

—Should I tell Candace?

—Why didn't you tell her when she was a kid?

—Milt never wanted to. It would have meant talking about things he still found . . . very painful. Trying to explain why he and Phil fought for the Loyalists. Why a lot of their friends called them traitors to their country. Why her natural father committed suicide . . .

—And why her natural mother walked away and left her.

—Yes, that, too. I think the real reason Milt called L.K. was to talk to her . . . about Candace.

That made sense. He could have stopped the killings by just saying a word about L.K. to Candy or me.

—When it looked like the Agency was going to blame Milt for the killings and Candace would suffer, I thought I should tell her the truth. Now . . . I don't know. Should I?

Hell, I ain't Ann Landers. Who am I to give anybody advice on how to handle secrets from the past? I did a piss poor job with my own. I carried Camille around in my head for twenty years. And I wasn't sure yet if the best part of me wasn't buried with her and Danny in Forest Lawn.

—You gotta decide that, I said. —But I'd think long and hard on it before I did.

After a while, Candy come in, dressed in black but not mourning. Her smile warmed the room. Seems Narbonne had put in a good word for her after all. She had reason to hope the Agency meant to forgive and forget Milt Hebron's past. They'd ordered her back to Washington. She had a flight scheduled for that afternoon.

Elaine Prescott pecked my cheek as we left and whispered she did mean to think on it before saying anything to Candy. On the way to the parking lot, Candy and I compared schedules and found we had a couple of hours to spare before making it out the 405 to LAX.

—I could help you pack, Candy offered.

—I checked out before I come looking for you, I said.

—Too bad. I'll always have fond memories of that room at the Hollywood Roosevelt. It's right up there with the one we shared at the Goldenes Kreuz. How about we stop by Mother's house? There's a sinful-red Jacuzzi we could make new memories in.

Now what kind of man turns down that kind of invitation? Only a man with another good-bye to say.

—Thanks, honey, but I got another date.

Her eyes chilled, and she looked hurt for a moment. —Is this Germany all over again?

—There's one big difference. This time I'm headed out to Forest Lawn.

She bit her lip, then asked real soft, —May I come with you?

—If you want to.

—I want to. I really do.

There's a timeless quality about California. The native trees are evergreen, the weather never seems to change. The sun is always bright, the air crisp. It's like you've already entered Paradise without the inconvenience of dying.

When I bought two heart-shaped wreaths of roses at the florist, Candy looked curious.

—The second's for Danny, I explained.

—Danny Bynum, Camille's son?

—Mine, too.

—Oh, Rat . . . I'm sorry. I never knew.

—I didn't either, till it was too late.

I was surprised when a guard stopped us at the entrance to Forest Lawn and asked for identification. Did we look like grave robbers? The guard was apologetic.

—Former President Reagan is expected to attend a service today, he explained, pointing up the long drive in the direction of a distant canopy over a newly opened grave.

We drove past a line of limos. Dark-suited men wearing sunglasses, with mikes on their lapels and wires in their ears, were out at the edge of the crowd of mourners who were making their way to their seats.

—It's Congressman Bearden's funeral, Candy said. —Al must be working today.

Camille's grave was not far away. The mountain of flowers that had covered it at her funeral had been removed. There are no wilted flowers in Paradise. The sod had been replaced, and the ground looked almost undisturbed. Death made only a small impression on the green, rolling expanse of Forest Lawn.

I lay the wreaths side by side, remembering a wise child who sang a sad song, and his beautiful mother who wanted the world but ended up with only a small plot of earth. The red roses melted and ran like bleeding hearts. I looked away to clear my eyes.

A motorcade of four limos was entering the gate and moving toward the Bearden grave site. The early-arriving mourners were all seated now, awaiting Reagan's appearance. The drivers of the parked limos stood a respectful distance away, talking quietly among themselves. One looked up, saw me, waved, and hurried over.

—Hi, Mr. Trapp, Leslie said. —I thought you'd be back in New Orleans by now.

—I'm almost on my way. You toting for the Bearden funeral?

—No, I was just talking to some of the guys who are. The little old lady I brought out to her husband's grave wanted to be alone.

Leslie gestured at a distant figure in black. There's nothing suspicious about a widow visiting her husband's grave. But something about her tickled the back of my neck, tensed those muscles.

—Did your lady know where the grave was she wanted to visit?

—No, I had to ask directions at the office.

—What's the name of the deceased?

—Stern. Philip Stern.

—My God, Candy breathed, and fumbled in her purse.

I broke into a flat-out run toward the four-car motorcade, which was just pulling to a stop at the Bearden grave. That almost got me shot. I saw at least six dark suits throw down on me. I started yelling at the top of my voice.

—Narbonne . . . Al Narbonne . . .

He was already out of the front car and turning toward me as he heard his name. Al recognized me and yelled out to the other agents.

—Don't shoot. He's all right. . . .

—Get your man out of here, I shouted.

He hesitated. —What the hell . . . ?

—I was wrong, I yelled. —L.K. wants Reagan, too.

He still didn't understand, but that was enough for Narbonne. He signaled the drivers, —Go, go. . . .

Car doors slammed, and the four limos peeled off at an undignified speed as Narbonne ran to meet me.

—What have you found out?

—I don't know what she's planned, but L.K.'s here.

Narbonne's years of security paid off. He thought of something I hadn't. —Get those people away from the grave, he yelled at the dark suits. —Tell 'em don't wait for their cars. Move 'em.

With shouts and prods, his people began herding the mourners away from the grave. And hardly a second too soon.

With a loud, dull roar and a belch of flame, the Bearden coffin exploded. The fleeing people were knocked down by the impact. Then loose dirt and flowers began raining down from heaven on the screaming crowd like God had decided to bury them all alive where they lay.

I didn't stop to help anybody. Others could do that. I was already running toward the woman in black, with Narbonne chuffing hard behind me.

Only there was no need to hurry. When we reached her, L.K. was just a huddle of black clothes, like the wicked witch in *The Wizard of Oz*.

Candy stood over her, her 9mm in her hand. She looked at us with a mixture of defiance and pride.

—I told her I was a federal officer. To put up her hands. She went for a weapon.

But when Narbonne unfolded L.K.'s withered hand, she wasn't clutching a gun. Though it was a deadly weapon of sorts. The metal thing in her hand was a remote controller. She'd used it to set off a charge that had been planted in Bearden's coffin, or maybe in the open grave under it. Since Candy's slug had blown a hole through L.K.'s chest, I didn't reckon we'd ever find out exactly how she'd managed that.

—Well, honey, I said, —I guess you just evened the score for your daddy.

—It wasn't that way, she protested. —I thought she was going for a gun. I fired in self-defense.

—And that's how the report will read, Narbonne stated flatly. —Don't worry. This isn't going to hurt your record one bit. You'll probably get a commendation.

Candy looked real pleased at that. That's what a dozen years with the Agency does for you. It makes you feel good about doing your patriotic duty and killing your own mother. If I ever shared a brandy with Jacobs again, I'd have to tell him how this all come out. He'd laugh his ass off.

I looked down with something like pity at L.K.'s frail old body. She was lying stretched across a granite footmarker. The blood pumped out by her dying heart almost covered what had been carved there: Philip Stern, 1915–1951. A thin black veil wrapped her face, softening her ravaged features. In death, she looked younger, more peaceful. Maybe because, at long last, she was embracing her lover.